DODGING RED CLOUD

RICHARD S. WHEELER

SAGEBRUSH
Large Print Westerns

First published in Great Britain by ISIS Publishing Ltd.
First published in the United States by
M. Evans and Company, Inc.

First Isis Edition
published 2016
by arrangement with
Golden West Literary Agency

A catalogue record for this book is available
from the British Library.

ISBN 978–1–78541–218–9 (pb)

Published by
F. A. Thorpe (Publishing)
Anstey, Leicestershire

Set by Words & Graphics Ltd.
Anstey, Leicestershire
Printed and bound in Great Britain by
T. J. International Ltd., Padstow, Cornwall

This book is printed on acid-free paper

To Ray and Barbara Puechner

CHAPTER
ONE

She watched the distant blue-clad troopers angle toward her and knew she would have to stop. She knew what they would say and how she would reply. She tugged the reins to bring the roan mare to a stop and waited in her enameled green buckboard for the soldiers to arrive.

They were the last obstacle. Then she would escape this wilderness forever. She adjusted her bonnet. She despised bonnets — they made her look like an immigrant wife — but they were necessary in this hot August sun. Her creamy complexion was her best feature — that and other assets — and she didn't intend to burn it.

She was tempted to make a run for Bozeman Pass and freedom. If she did, the soldiers might simply give up the chase. There was nothing they could do, anyway. She glanced behind her. Everything was neatly tied down in the buckboard: her tent, food, Henry carbine, the four-shot lady revolver, spare clothes, bedroll, two canteens, and all the rest.

The three cavalry troopers were loping now and would be angling up to her soon. Let them come, then. She'd be all smiles, which was something she was practiced at. She pulled her bonnet off and let her auburn hair cascade, glinting in the high sun. These soldiers would be no different from all the men of Virginia City, who loved her wry smile and sweet voice. She wore a dress that was as revealing of her assets as it was demure, in bottle-green velveteen to match her eyes. It was a dress made for social occasions rather than life along the Bozeman Trail, but she had put it on today for this occasion. And after she got past Fort Ellis she'd put on something more practical and cool.

Ahead of her rose the Bridger Mountains and Bozeman Pass, and beyond that, the Yellowstone Valley, the great northern prairies . . . and Red Cloud.

A lieutenant hailed her and she was glad. It was one thing to be halted by an enlisted man, quite another to be halted by an officer. She smiled prettily, her eyes upon his shoulder bar, and finally upon his face. He was flanked by two troopers whose features she didn't notice. The man she did notice had straight ebony hair, a hawk-beak nose, and cold gray eyes that she could see were surveying her from top to bottom.

She wiggled slightly and grinned.

"Where are you headed, madam?" he asked at last.

"Saratoga Springs, New York."

"Nice place to go if you can get there," he said thoughtfully. "But you can't. The trail's closed and we're stopping all traffic."

"Red Cloud?" she asked.

"The same and more. A lot more. The Army's pulling out. We've abandoned Fort C. F. Smith and

Fort Phil Kearny. It'll be Sioux and Cheyenne country soon, if it isn't already."

"Well, that's nice. I hope they enjoy it," she replied.

He pondered a moment. "I suppose I should ask what a lady like you is doing out here in a dangerous wilderness all alone."

"Going to Saratoga Springs." She dimpled her cheeks.

"Where are you coming from?"

"Virginia City."

He mulled that over too. "You should have gone around. And you need an escort."

Going around meant a long loop west and south through Idaho and Wyoming country until she struck the Oregon Trail.

"I always take the shortest route between two points," she said. "And I always take whatever risks are worthwhile."

"I can see that," he muttered. "At any rate, you're not going. Army has instructions to stop all traffic."

"I guess I'll just have to stop at Fort Ellis, then."

He scratched the side of his nose. "Your presence would illuminate the post, madam."

"Miss, not madam. I'm single." She tore the glove off her left hand, letting him see the bare ring finger but not letting him know that the finger would always be bare, for she had no intention of every marrying.

She looked into his eager face and glanced at the enlisted men as well, knowing the effect she had on them.

"Let's go to the fort. I'm simply delighted to make your acquaintance. And, of course, I'll want to pay my respects to your general in charge."

She wheeled her mare and steered her buckboard out of the deep ruts of the trail. They escorted her not altogether solemnly to the new fort, which stood as a buffer now between the hostiles and the western mining camps.

"His name is Marcus Aurelius Fox. He's a colonel. And I'm Lieutenant Timothy Swanson."

"Delighted, and I am Hannah Holt."

Fort Ellis was a crude affair, only half built, barely a year old. Rough log buildings encompassed a dusty parade ground baking in the August sun. She steered toward the squat log structure with the flagpole in front of it.

"I'll find the colonel," said Lieutenant Swanson.

The parade ground was deserted, with scarcely a soldier in sight. Nothing moved, not even the horses pastured in the tawny foothills to the south and east. How dreary and asleep the frontier was, she thought, and how bright and active Saratoga Springs would be. The enlisted men had vanished and she was alone.

Then Colonel Marcus Aurelius Fox materialized in the doorway, wearing cavalry britches, suspenders, and red long johns.

"My lord, a lady," he exclaimed, and yawned. "Siesta time. My apologies for . . . this state of dishabille."

He had a white, bald, jowly face and peered at her from behind spectacles with round lenses and steel rims.

4

"My lord, a *real* lady."

"You look just dashing, Captain," she said prettily.

"Ah . . . it's colonel," said the lieutenant as he made the introductions. They invited Hannah in for tea.

"I've been sitting for hours. I think I'll stand," she said. She was a tall woman, and standing would allow them to enjoy her. She didn't broach the topic of travel until a half hour of niceties had elapsed and their delight had grown. Men did that. They gradually expanded in her presence. When she judged that their inflation had proceeded far enough, she began.

"Marcus, dear, I really must be heading east before the weather turns. My mother's ill . . . and my intended is waiting for me . . ."

"Miss Holt, that's impossible. At least on the Bozeman Trail."

"But of course it is!" she said, noting the sudden and entirely true-to-form sadness in their eyes. "I'm going to take the Bridger cutoff. I won't even be in Sioux country. It isn't so far from here to the cutoff, and if there are Indians, they'll be friendly Crows. And once I'm at the cutoff and heading down the Big Horn River, maybe Shoshone too. That's what everybody says."

"Well, no, miss. It is not safe for an unescorted lady. There are renegades. There are Sioux raiding parties even west of the Big Horn Mountains. And not all of the Crow and Shoshone are reliably friendly. You'd be in grave danger the whole time."

"Oh, pshaw! You worry too much! In Virginia City they said that Red Cloud never came this far west. Lives over in Dakota."

The colonel rubbed a hand over his white, bald skull.

"Red Cloud goes wherever he goes, miss. Do you have any idea — Miss Holt, there's blood and death and mutilation and murder out there. The Bloody Bozeman — that's what this road is called. For years this chief, this brilliant, obsessed Oglala war leader, along with the Minneconjou and Sitting Bull's Hunkpapa and that young fanatic Crazy Horse — for years they've butchered helpless immigrants along that trail. The man looks like Abe Lincoln without the beard, but he's no Lincoln. He's a butcher. The Powder River country is their prime hunting land, the Yellowstone country is their prime buffalo land, and he'll defend both to the death. I confess he's succeeded so far. He's the first Indian in history to win a war with the U.S. Army. At least for now . . ."

Hannah had heard all this before, and she listened impatiently. She was going east, and nothing would stop her, including wild Indians.

"The Army pulled out of Fort C. F. Smith a few weeks ago — and it was burned. Now we're leaving Phil Kearny — and they'll burn *it*. And Reno. Red Cloud said he won't even show up at Fort Laramie for treaty talk until the Army has left and every white has been driven out. We can't protect — we don't have the money or men to protect that road. So we're abandoning it. Once you go over this pass into that country, you're a dead woman. Oh, maybe not at once, but every tick of the clock, every sunset, every dawn

6

will take you closer to a violent death — or worse, in your case, being, ah, young and attractive . . ."

"Well, I'll be careful. What I really want, dear man, is an escort."

"Escort? We're prohibited from —"

"You can escort me to the east end of the pass."

"And then?"

"Then I'll just be on my merry way."

"Along the Yellowstone, through country without a white man in it?"

"That's right." She lifted her chin. "I'll take my chances. I believe in going where I'm going and not turning back to drive an extra four or five hundred miles."

"You're an amazing lady, Miss Holmes."

"Holt. Hannah Holt."

"Oh, yes, excuse me. I'll remember your name for the burial lists."

She glanced around the austere headquarters with its whitewashed log walls. "I do love the cavalry," she said with a sigh. "All you brave men in blue. I'd love to see you on dress parade."

"Parade? Here?" The colonel looked shocked.

"Why, yes. All dressed up with sabers shining and flags flying and marching for me with the regimental band playing."

"We have no band," said Lieutenant Swanson.

"Then ride for me, all in a row. How I'd love that! I will wear a yellow ribbon for you."

Colonel Fox rubbed his stubbled cheek and then polished his bald head until she thought it would turn shiny. "Haven't had a dress parade since leaving Fort Abe Lincoln," he muttered.

"Then have one for me. And then escort me as far east as you can, through the pass. And then leave me, and I'll just waltz along."

"You are a lady with peculiar notions."

"Well, I just adore soldiers." She batted her eyelids twice for emphasis.

Colonel Marcus Aurelius Fox muttered to himself and scratched his bristly jowls. "I suppose if we turned you west, the way you came, you'd just give us the slip, anyway, and go through at night."

"Oh. I won't dream of it, Colonel. What I want is your cooperation. I tell you what. Let's have a ball. All the officers — and me. We'll dance tonight, and tomorrow we'll all go over the pass."

"Now that's a fine idea," said Timothy Swanson. "There are four officers here and no wives, and you'll be belle of the ball."

"Now see here, Mr. Swanson, we have no music."

"Yes, we do, sir. Sergeant Eddie McDowell plays the fiddle."

Hannah brightened. "And I have two bottles of French champagne in my buckboard," she cried.

"I don't know about noncoms at an officers' ball," Marcus Aurelius Fox muttered. "I suppose . . . if he behaves himself."

And it was done.

"Miss Holt, delighted to have you. Dinner at seven. Ball following."

She smiled.

"Swanson, show Miss Holt to the William Tecumseh Sherman room. Alert Cookie. Tell Eddie McDowell to bring his fiddle."

"Delighted, simply delighted, Colonel Fox. You're going to such trouble, and all for me."

Fox studied her. "Women are scarce here. And I am ignoring my better judgment."

By late afternoon the post had come alive. Woodcutting details returned along with fencing and horse-care details. Three mounted patrols came in, unsaddled, cared for their mounts, and then drifted to the barracks.

Hannah combed her auburn hair until it shone; donned her green silk ball gown, which was scooped low in front; added an ivory cameo on a black velvet choker; and dabbed a bit if lilac perfume behind her ears. It was a pity there was no looking glass in which she could admire herself, but no matter.

Promptly at seven, three spit-and-polished junior officers appeared. Lieutenant Swanson did the honors. "This is Captain Chilton Wolf and Captain Christopher Brent."

She caressed each one with her eyes. They beamed.

At the newly completed officers' mess they banqueted and toasted Hannah with her champagne. At the head of the table sat Marcus Aurelius Fox. At his left, the guest of honor. Next to her and across, Captains Wolf and Brent. The lieutenant was banished to the nether end.

"Now, Miss Holt —" began the colonel.

"Call me Hannah, dear man."

"Now, Hannah. You must tell us how it is that a lady of your, uh, attributes is wandering through a dangerous wilderness in a buckboard all alone."

She knew it was coming, and her cheeks dimpled. She loved to smile at just one man, and she chose Captain Wolf, who was portly and phlegmatic and twitched whenever she peered into his wet brown eyes.

"Why," she began, "I got rich in Virginia City. All those nice men . . . It was real estate, not gold. I simply bought lots and hired woodcutters and carpenters to build buildings, then rented the buildings, and it was amazing how much money I made."

That wasn't quite accurate, she thought, but it'd do. She rarely rented. She offered her buildings for a quarter or a third of the receipts. Only when she didn't trust the proprietors did she rent, and the rentals were high.

"Ah," exclaimed Chilton Wolf, "you've only added to the mystery about you, Hannah! A lone woman in a wild mining camp, building and renting to —"

"Hardware dealers, mercantiles, a livery, a harness maker, a hotel, a boardinghouse . . ."

She let the rest go. Twenty of her twenty-seven buildings had been occupied by saloons, sporting parlors, dance halls, certain other female enterprises she blanked from her mind, and one Chinese opium den.

"Oh, yes," she added, "a saddlery and a daguerreotypist who made the sweetest portrait of me reclining on a sofa in, ah, dishabille. Such a dear little man."

The colonel piped up, "How on earth, Miss Holt —"

10

"Call me Hannah. Hard-hearted Hannah."

He chucked appreciatively. "How on earth did you do all that alone? Were you, uh, married?"

She sighed tenderly. "Goodness, no. I met such nice men, fatherly men, at the church socials and box lunches. Whoever got my box lunch, why, I soon had a new friend. And they were all so helpful, lending me money and good solid business advice. My, I had so many dear friends . . ."

"But alone? How did you ever get there in the first place?" inquired Captain Brent.

"Oh, dear, that's a long story. I was engaged, and my intended went to Virginia City to make his fortune. Soon he summoned me from my dear home in upstate New York, and so I went, but he had died of consumption the week before I arrived after a long and harrowing journey . . . so there I was . . . It was very sad."

"Indeed. And a woman alone thrown to the wolves," said Wolf.

"Fortunately," said Hannah testily, "I had a small nest egg. There are such dangers, you know, such temptations, such pits to fall into, where a woman's tenderness and virtue count for nothing. Well, thank God I was able to avoid them all. My prayers were answered and soon I was in business!"

"But if you were doing so well, why have you left?" asked Lieutenant Swanson.

Hannah fixed the young man with her jade-green eyes and sighed, a world of sadness in her golden face, neck, and breast. She sighed again.

"Well, that's a long story too. I suppose I can be brief, though. This frontier, the wild camps . . . well, you know they aren't a proper place for nice girls. I mean, it's all so crude and new, and the class of people here . . . surely you understand. I grew up in, well, gentle circumstances, you know, and this wild place is just — not what I want. And also the men, dear as they were, they all had domestic plans for me . . . ah, marriage, since I was the only lady of, ah, my kind, in the camp almost. Of course, there were lots of the other kind, and I understand the need for them, poor things. But it was so sad. I had no wish to stay there or break people's hearts. They'd ask and I'd say no, and they'd leave crestfallen and with tears in their strong male eyes. I just couldn't cope with that. It was such a tragedy."

She sipped her champagne. "And of course I have a few dollars now, and it's safely banked in New York. So I'm returning to the gentle life I want."

That would do, she thought. She said nothing about her plans to become the belle of the spa and casino at Saratoga Springs, or the racehorses she intended to own.

And so it went. The dishes were cleared. Master Sergeant Eddie McDowell — a man built like a top — was brought in, and they waltzed and gavotted for two hours more, and when she begged leave around midnight, two captains and a lieutenant were in love and a colonel in lust.

She bid them adieu, hugged each of them sweetly, kissed them gently on their cheeks, and hoped they'd have the honor of escorting her over Bozeman Pass and down to the Yellowstone the next day.

So, she thought in bed, they wouldn't stop her. They never did. Almost never.

When they got to the bottom of the pass, she'd try to entice them further. That would be tougher because it meant disobeying orders and entering Indian country. But she had a way with men . . . even Army men.

CHAPTER
TWO

The next morning, when Hannah emerged from the officers' mess after breakfasting, she discovered her buckboard awaiting her. The roan mare had been brushed, the axles greased, the harness oiled. Miraculously the wooden seat had acquired quilted leather padding, and an Army canvas poncho-bedroll had been added to her gear.

She beamed. The junior officers grinned. And she kissed them all.

But just beyond was an even more compelling sight, a full company, a troop, mounted and at the ready, and led by Colonel Marcus Aurelius Fox himself. It wasn't exactly a dress parade — in fact, there weren't enough dress blues to go around at this raw, new post — but it was close. The cavalry britches had been brushed. Horse and tack shone. At the head of the column the flag and yellow guidons fluttered. Colonel Fox wore a silver-sheathed saber and twin pearl-handled Colt Army revolvers. And a hundred pair of longing eyes were upon her.

Hannah remembered the biblical verses about seeking and finding, asking and receiving. That was how to live — ask and receive.

14

They escorted her over the pass in a long column, two by two. The colonel rode at her side and sometimes drove the buckboard itself, furtively eyeing the voluptuous figure that was now encased in the bottle-green velveteen again. By evening they had descended to the plains, to the valley of the Yellowstone, and had bivouacked beside the cold river right at the great bend where it emerged from the land of the geysers to swing east toward the great Missouri River. They pitched her tent for her, ringed their bedrolls in a great circle around her, and then cooked evening mess.

She dined with the officers, then gently proposed that they escort her farther.

"Miz Holt, we'd accompany you all the way to Saratoga Spring if we could. But we can't," said Colonel Fox. And that was the end of that.

In the morning they gave her a yellow ribbon, and she tied it around her auburn locks, making a ponytail. Then she shook a hundred hands and broke a hundred hearts and rode down to the crossing of the Yellowstone, which she negotiated easily while they watched. Then they mounted and were gone.

It was quiet. The wheels hummed along on their newly greased axles. The roan mare's steady clopping was all the noise there was, except for the cawing of some crows. It was peaceful, too, in the warm sun. But most of all it was empty. She felt terribly alone, though not unsafe. Not in this furthermost corner of Indian country, where she was far from the raiding Sioux.

There were cottonwood copses along the chilly river, and at one of these she lunched. She took off her green velveteen dress, which had been hot, and which she didn't want to get trail-grimed, and slipped into a checked blue gingham more suitable for the summer heat. She wished she had a male audience. They would be such a comfort.

She let the mare graze while she munched a slab of beef the soldiers had given her. A burlap bag of beans had been added to her gear too. She despised red beans but was glad to have the food for emergencies.

This wilderness was a bleak, alarming place, and she felt its suffocation upon her. There would be no escape. Just day after day of plodding until Fort Laramie, and then some more plodding — she wasn't sure how far — to the Union Pacific tracks or to the railhead, wherever that was.

Today was the first day of September 1868. She supposed the last part of the long trek would be chilly. In Virginia City the winters were early and ferocious. But now it was so balmy that she was sure the weather would hold for a while.

For two days she drove east in silence, not encountering a soul, though she passed some abandoned places where white men had settled and then left. It unnerved her, this vast, empty land. In her sweet voice she sang everything she could think of, and hymns such as "Amazing Grace," and "Rock of Ages," and "Nearer My God to Thee." She passed fresh graves and they alarmed her. Cold gray clay and no grass on top. Only one was marked, and that woman had died in May. Had the Sioux come here, too, this far west?

The reality of it alarmed her. It was easy enough to imagine this trip in the safety of her Virginia City home: to plan for it, buy the things they told her she would need, and proceed with the whole thing in utmost secrecy, slowly selling her holdings and sending credit drafts east. But it was quite another to be here alone in a land without protection, in country now possessed by coppery natives who would kill her and rip the auburn hair from her scalp — or worse, enslave her for lustful purposes.

That evening she apologized to God for all the money she had made as a silent partner in dubious enterprises and told Him she'd turn over to charity all she had earned from her twenty-five percent interest in Madam Marie Antoinette's House of Royal Pleasure.

And then she turned to what she knew of survival on the trail. For months she'd pumped her frontier friends about it. And now she applied them. The tiny Indian-style fire she built — her instincts ran to huge bonfires — was in a protected hollow in a cottonwood grove. The leaves would dissipate the smoke, and the terrain itself, so carefully selected, cupped the firelight. The buckboard, too, was invisible, deep in shadow. The roan mare was picketed in a little clearing surrounded by river brush. She pitched her tent near the dwindling fire but chose instead to spread her bedroll in the shadows beyond — also against her deepest instincts. She kept her Henry repeater with her always.

She slept fitfully, alarmed once by the coyotes barking their carnival in the hills. In the morning she was tired and melancholy, angry that she hadn't trusted anyone enough to hire an escort. It was different here; there was a strange, lurking menace that didn't exist when she camped along the trail between Virginia City, Bozeman Pass, and Fort Ellis.

The new day was a little different. Now there were high herringbone clouds here and there, and she had some vague recollection that such clouds presaged a turn in the weather. She eyed the Army poncho gratefully as she harnessed the mare.

In many places the great ruts of the trail took her out of sight of the Yellowstone as she continued east. But the trail was the work of some genius, for always it wheeled around the easiest slopes, so that the mare rarely labored up hard grades.

That noon she hid in a grove of willows and ate more beef and washed in a creek. It was a chilly day, and to the west a gray cloud mass loomed, and the peaks to the south caught towering columns of white. She knew Montana Territory and knew how summers turned into winters in minutes; sometimes winters turned into summers just as fast. She pulled out her mackinaw. It wouldn't shed water, but the army poncho over it would.

There was no place to shelter. She thought she might pitch her tent but decided to go on. Every step east was a step toward civilization. The mare perked up in the fresher weather and jogged effortlessly.

The sun disappeared in a gray haze, and the temperature plunged twenty degrees in moments. She donned the mackinaw and kept on going. It did not rain. She drove through the gray afternoon with the overcast sawing off the tops of the mountains to the south. Later in the day the trail curved close to the bank of the Yellowstone, which was wide and braided and shallow here, and Hannah knew she had come to the place on the crude maps where the Boulder River flowed in from the south, and where the trail cut southeast, never to touch the Yellowstone again.

The mare stood uncertainly at the edge of the crossing. It was dry season, and the Boulder River seemed low and slow and safe. She snapped her whip, and the mare slowly tugged the buckboard across and safely up the flat grade on the far side. The water had never reached the floorboards. She was grateful for that but angry with herself for forgetting something. Part of the trail lore she had learned from all those dear men was to study all crossings awhile for the possibility of an ambush, for surprises.

And then it rained. The drops stung like cold needles. There was nothing here, no shelter at all. The trail wound up the Boulder valley a bit, and she hunted for anything like a ledge or overhang to get under. But these were wide, grassy flats with barren hills to either side. She rode miserably a half mile more, and then, in the distance, rising from the foggy dark, were log buildings. She made out a large cabin, a low log barn, and corrals. She slapped her reins over the mare, put her into a fast trot, and wheeled into the place. It was deserted. She remembered, too late, that the same rule applied here as with river crossings: Study it first.

Still, it was obviously abandoned. It had that look. No doubt the owner left when the army left. The rain lashed down in icy sheets now, and she steered straight for the barn and drove through its open door. It was gloomy there, almost black, and the mare was instantly restless, rolling her eyes, tensing up. Hannah felt only relief to be out of the pelting cold.

She put the mare in a box stall. There was no hay, but there was a scythe near the door, and the bottomland weeds here were thick. Later, she thought, she'd cut enough for the roan. The mare acted crazy, but Hannah ignored her, dug through her supplies, and dashed for the cabin. The door wouldn't open. She kicked it. Then she spotted a latchstring and pulled it. A bar inside lifted, and the door swung open easily. It was dank and dark inside, and something, probably a pack rat, scurried through the room. She waited for her eyes to adjust. On the far wall she noticed a fieldstone and mudmortar fireplace. That was good. But there was no kindling; indeed, the place was starkly empty save for a crude table and chairs and some blackened kitchen supplies on a shelf.

Hannah pulled on the canvas poncho and plunged into the twilight. There was no kindling or firewood in the barn, either. But through the sleeting rain she spotted a shed beyond the barn. Surely the owner of this place had firewood somewhere! This was Montana Territory! The shed had no door, and inside, on pegs, hung all manner of harnesses — bridle reins,

20

bellybands, hames, collars, oxbows, and more. And in a corner a pile of dry, forgotten sticks. She gathered a bundle, intending to start her fire and then hunt for something more substantial. On her way back to the cabin she discovered a whole pile of wood under the rear eaves of the cabin where she hadn't looked. Quickly she struck steel across flint, sending a shower of tiny stars into a thimble-sized pile of shavings, and soon had her blaze. The heat felt soothing. But before she changed into dry clothes, she'd feed the mare. She found the scythe and swung it awkwardly through purplish weeds. She cut two wet armfuls, dumped them in the manger, and fled to the cabin, shivering. The rain had become sleet.

It felt so secure here. She relaxed as the cabin warmed. Surely there would be no hostile Indians around on a night like this . . . and yet that possibility never left her. She wondered who had lived here, two or three hundred yards off the Bozeman Road. Not a woman, surely. Whoever owned it had fled with most of his goods. He must have made his living from the Bozeman Road.

She thought she heard something outside and grabbed her Henry. She had become passably good with it, under the tutoring of several beaux back in Virginia City. She slid the door open a crack.

Nothing.

The night was quiet. She closed the door and dropped the bolt and pulled in the latchstring. She must remember, she thought, not to lock herself out in the morning. It seemed a fortress here, but a fortress that would last about as long as it took a flaming arrow to ignite a log wall.

She imagined that she heard things outside again but blamed her all-too-vivid imagination. She eyed the bed dubiously. It was a rough-hewn frame with a tight cross weave of rawhide straps. She was sure a tick belonged on top, but she had none and wondered about sleeping on the straps with only her bedroll. The packed earth floor looked even less inviting.

There was a knock.

No knock in all her life had jolted her so badly. She froze in disbelief, then terror. The knock came again, louder. It was the last thing she expected. She was in a vast, empty wilderness; there were no people here!

She clutched her Henry and raised it.

The banging continued.

"Open up, lady," said a high voice.

English! It wasn't an Indian ... or was it? A half-breed?

"Hey, open up."

"What do you want?"

"I want to meet who's crazy enough to light fires in there."

She did nothing, undecided. Then she lifted the heavy bolt and opened the door a crack. Standing outside in the gloom was a boy. She stared. He had a rifle, but it wasn't aimed. She let him in.

The flickering fire revealed a skinny, hard-eyed lad, perhaps twelve or thirteen. The boy had a long, thin-nosed face laced with freckles poking out of a ragged and filthy shirt that was tucked into even more ragged dungarees. He was barefoot.

"What are you doing here?" she asked lamely.

"Same as you, I guess. Dodging Red Cloud."

"You must be cold."

"Sure am, only I wasn't so dumb to build a fire. I was in the barn. I put your mare out on the pasture. That brown snakeweed yuh gave her she wouldn't eat."

"Snakeweed?"

"Yeah. They don't eat snakeweed or gumweed. They can't swallow it."

"Oh . . . but won't my mare wander away?"

"Naw. Buck fence around that pasture."

The boy was a comfort.

"Well, come and warm yourself. I have some roast beef. What's your name?

"Linc Larrimer."

"Linc?"

"Yeah, like the president. My ma and pa are dead. The Sioux got them over near the Big Horns. I was out rabbit hunting and they missed me. Wish I was there; I'd'a shot them to bits. Who are yuh?"

"I'm Hannah Holt, and I'm on my way east. I'll take the Bridger Cutoff when I get there. That'll be safer . . ."

"Yuh are crazy, lady. What do yuh do? Are yuh a widder or something?"

"No, I have businesses."

"Yuh run one of them places that have ladies?"

"Goodness, no!"

"Too bad. Yuh look like yuh should. That's where I'm going. Virginia City. That's where Ma and Pa were going."

She handed him a slab of army beef on a tin plate from her kit. He devoured it, saying nothing.

"If I see that Red Cloud, I'm gonna kill him," he said. "Yuh got anything I can wear? My feet are freezing."

"Your feet are too large —"

"I need something fast. The Sioux, they got my folks and left me a naked orphan, almost. I'll get even. When I get some shoes and a horse and some bullets, I'm going to git him."

"Get him?"

"Git that Red Cloud. I'll ride right in and plug him. No one will suspect a boy."

"That's not very practical."

"It beats being an orphan."

She watched him speculatively as he wolfed down the last of the beef. "Do you hunt?" she asked.

"I'm a good hunter. How do yuh think I stayed alive? Only I got three cartridges left now."

"I have a Henry and lots of cartridges, but I don't know how to hunt. If you were to come along with me —"

"Yuh going the wrong way, so I can't help."

"Why don't you come east with me? Two of us are stronger than one. And what's there for you in Virginia City, anyway?"

"I don't know. Gold, people, jobs. Maybe mucking out stalls in a livery barn. A place to sleep, anyway."

24

"There's more in the east. More if you came with me."

"Yeah, Red Cloud and Ma and Pa's bodies. I ran from there and didn't even stay to put them underground."

"Linc, we could really do —"

"I'm not gonna go near there."

She sighed. "Let's talk about it tomorrow. I'm tired. You'll have to stay in the barn, of course."

"The barn? It's freezing out there. Why?"

"Because I'm a respectable woman and I don't have men near me at night."

"Who says yuh are respectable? Yuh are too pretty."

She paused, burning. "I won't have you here."

"My ma was respectable and —"

"Married."

"I got cold feet."

"I'll lend you a canvas poncho."

"That's supposed to keep me warm?"

"If I hadn't arrived, you'd have nothing."

"Yah, and now we got a fire and smoke to attract Indians. If it wasn't raining, I'd put miles between me and you. But there ain't Indians going to come in the rain."

She smiled sweetly. "In the morning, Linc, I'll help you. We'll make something for your feet, and maybe I'll give you the poncho."

He was reluctant to leave. "Well, I'll be safer out there than yuh are with this here fire. Gimme the poncho."

She let him out, closed and bolted the door.

CHAPTER
THREE

It was drizzling the next day, and that meant the chances of Indian trouble were lessened. But Linc demanded that she let the fire die, anyway, and reluctantly she did.

They found a piece of tanned elk skin in the shed where the harness was. Some of it had been cut into reins and thong. With an awl they found there and Linc's skinning knife, they fashioned some crude moccasins and cut a pair of spare soles. From the ragged remains of a saddle blanket they made some inner liners and some leggings. The boy would need a lot more clothing fast, but there was nothing left in the place, and Hannah would not part with any of her own except the army poncho.

Beyond the pasture where the mare grazed, a herd of antelope was scattered along the slopes. Linc shot one, waited a long time to see whether the shot would bring trouble, and then dragged the heavy carcass to the barn. They would have meat for their supper, but he was more interested in the hide, which he peeled off carefully, fleshed as best he could, and then rubbed with a mixture of brains and liver. There would be no time for real tanning, so he beat the hide with a club, hoping to pound the stiffness out of it. It was an afternoon's labor.

Late in the day the rain stopped. Linc walked up the east slope of the valley until he could see out over the plains. He saw nothing. No movement. The whole world was soaked and silent. Tomorrow would be warm and sunny again — and more dangerous.

At dusk Hannah risked a tiny, hot, and almost smokeless fire in the hearth and set the antelope steaks to roasting. She slipped outside to observe. What little smoke there was rose straight up in the windless air, its color impossible to discern from the gray overcast.

She wanted to take the boy east with her — he'd add to her safety. But she didn't know how to induce him. The boy had a mean tongue; he seemed to jeer at her. But he'd be useful, and that was all that mattered. She wondered what on earth she might say to persuade him . . . He was just a boy, after all. Or was he? And then she knew. The things that had always worked for her among men — beauty, the promise of delicious things on the horizon — would work with Linc. How old was he? Thirteen or so? That was enough.

He walked in angrily. "This place is a trap. I'm gonna eat and then go," he announced.

"No one will come tonight."

"That's what Ma and Pa thought. No one would come. By morning we could be surrounded by Sioux. All they got to see is your horse."

They ate in silence. The antelope was half raw, not very good, and hard to chew. The buck had been an old one.

"I'll put out the fire soon. You can stay in here tonight, Linc. It's warmer."

"I always knew yuh'd let me, but I'm gonna go."

"The mare's grazed all day. We can put her in the barn now. No one will see her there. We can leave in the morning. Besides, Linc, it's still cold. You'll be cold."

"This here place is a trap."

"Well, if you must . . . I thought we'd be safer together, is all."

"Nah, I'm safer alone."

She dimpled her cheeks. "You wouldn't help a maiden in distress? What kind of knight are you?"

"No kinda knight at all, lady. I'll just leave yuh up in your tower and get my tail out of here."

"Stay tonight! It's cold. Leave before dawn when it's still black out. You can sleep here — and then go."

He thought about that. A night of warmth. Off in the morning darkness . . .

"Yeah, I'll do that," he said. "It's a dumb idea, but I'll do it, anyway. You're dumb to go east, like you don't want to live or something. It's safe in the mining camps. That's what Pa said."

"And now he's dead."

"Yuh got a big mouth," he said, snarling.

She retreated for a while. Then she said, "Linc, you've been orphaned, and I'd like to be your mother as much as possible and give you love and caring and family . . ."

"No, yuh don't! Yuh don't even know what being a mother is. Yuh think with me along yuh'll be safer, but yuh won't. Yuh'd just get me killed."

28

"I don't know what makes you think such things!" she exclaimed. "I'm just trying —"

"To use me. I'm heading west, lady."

Smiling, she approached him and kissed him on the cheek. "You're a nice young man," she murmured.

"I don't care what I am."

He glared at her, uneasy with the intimacy. It was twilight and the fire had died out.

"You may have that bunk," she said. "I'm uncomfortable in it." She motioned toward the crude bedstead. He sat on the woven rawhide, bounced a bit.

"It's better than hard earth," he conceded, and rolled himself in the poncho.

Hannah spread her bedroll near the still warm hearth, resenting the invasion of her privacy. She undid her high-top shoes and unbuttoned the sleeves of her dress, but that was as far as she would go. She rolled into the double four-point blankets, knowing she'd never get used to hard floors or hard earth.

At about one in the morning the mare whinnied from the barn.

Linc bolted upright. "I'm getting out of here," he muttered.

"Wait!" said Hannah.

But Lincoln didn't. He eased to the door on cat feet, silently lifted the bar, and opened it a crack. It had cleared off. Stars winked. There was only silence, deep and disturbing. From the barn now came quiet nickering, horse socializing. Someone was here, he knew. Maybe redskins. Maybe the same Oglalas as killed his ma and pa. If so, this place was a tomb.

29

He slipped back to the bunk, rolled up the poncho, and picked up his carbine. Hannah, sitting up in her blankets, stared. It was almost pitch black.

"Nice to know yuh," Linc whispered, and slid silently into the night. He stood in the murky overhang of the cabin for a minute, letting his senses probe into the night. It was very quiet. The Big Dipper had arced its way well around the North Star. The Milky Way splashed across the zenith. There was too much light, he thought, even if the moon was down. The black hulk of the barn was clearly visible.

"You're no Sioux," said a quiet voice in the barn, so low and relaxed that Linc could barely hear it. "And no Crow, either. Hard to judge in this light, but I make you to be a white boy, not full-grown."

It paralyzed Linc. There were white renegades; he'd heard of them, true savages, out beyond the rim of law, preying on the helpless. Like pirates. His pa had spoken of them. He said nothing and slid toward the river, wondering when the bullet would come.

The mare nickered again. Linc wondered if he should get out now and get to the Boulder River. From there he could slip to the Yellowstone.

"Smart to say nothing. But it's all right, boy. I own this place. At least until they burn it."

Linc paused. He was trapped now. He had heard Hannah bolting the door after him. She would not hear the soft voice drifting from the black cave of the barn. Well, he thought, at least he could be less of a target, and he slid to the ground, prone.

"Smart lad," said the voice. "Lost in the grass now. But no need. I'm in the same pickle as you. I'll step out so you can see me. Just don't shoot. A shot might bring the whole Sioux nation down on us."

Linc saw a figure now, a hulk of a man in the blurry dark. Enough to shoot at, but the man was trusting him. It was enough. He stood.

"That's better," said the low voice. "Let's go into the barn and palaver a little."

Reluctantly Linc crept toward the man and got the impression of height.

"I'm Wiley Smart, livestock trader," the voice said. "A fair deal for everyone."

"I ain't nobody," Linc replied. "But yuh can call me Linc."

"Who's in the house?"

Linc hesitated. "Some old woman going east. Crazy as a loon. Thinks she'll be safe on the Bridger Cutoff."

Wiley Smart laughed.

They walked side by side into the blackness of the barn. There was another horse in there; Linc sensed it more than saw it.

"Noisy mare, isn't she?" asked Wiley.

"Yeah."

"She belongs to this woman? And the wagon?"

"Yeah."

"What belongs to you?"

"Only what I got. This poncho, which I'm sort of taking from her, this carbine, two cartridges, and a skinning knife."

"And where are you going?"

"Virginia City. That's where Ma and Pa was going before the Sioux got them."

"I see." A pause. "It's not safe here. I moved back to my line cabin in the mountains. I pushed all my stock up there too. They'll burn this house any day now. But I keep an eye on it from up there with my spyglass. Saw you."

"Why yuh staying around here?"

"It can't last. I figure the trail will open up soon. Folks back East won't stand for the army pulling out. So I'm waiting it out up there. I had a good business. Reoutfitted people on the trail, took in worn stock, traded fresh."

"This is Crow land, ain't it?"

"Crow, yes. But with the army out, it's Sioux. The Crow lost it when the dratted cavalry left."

"Well, nice to meet yuh. I'm going to Virginia City now, before they all jump this here place."

"Yeah, sure, kid. Keep your hair on."

Linc turned to leave.

"Hey, wait. What's her name in there?"

"Hannah somebody."

"Thanks, muh boy. Just remember, if it's a horse you need, Wiley Smart is the trader to see. Fair deal . . ."

Linc trudged off, angry. It would have been nice if the man had asked him to stick around. Not that he wanted to stick around. To them he'd just be a pest, that's all. An orphan.

The farther he walked, the angrier he got. He reached the Boulder River and started down it, paused, and sat down to think. It was inky here, and behind every shrub lurked an Injun.

"Madam?"

The soft voice from outside startled her.

"Linc? Is that you, Linc?"

"No, the boy lit out. I'm Wiley Smart. This establishment is mine. My road ranch."

"Your what?"

"Road ranch. I reoutfit people on the trail."

Hannah paused. "How do I know that? What do you want?"

"Lady, you're in my parlors."

"It wasn't anyone's — it was abandoned."

"Well," came the voice through the door, "you're welcome to stay. I like all my guests and customers to leave here happy. If you need a horse or help, just call on old Wiley Smart. A fair deal for everyone."

"Wait." She unbolted the door.

It was so dark, she could barely see him, but the bulk of a large man was there. She stared into the darkness.

"Come in," she said reluctantly. "I have a candle."

"Don't light it until I close the door. Are the shutters tight?" asked the melodic voice.

She found the candle in her kit, and her little revolver, too, which she slipped into her tumbled blankets.

"I have a match," he said, and struck it and lit the proffered candle.

He stared, his eyes growing large. Men's eyes always did that, she thought. Her modest dishabille, sleeves and bodice unbuttoned, hair loose, only added to the effect. She let him admire.

Wiley Smart was a tall, muscular man with straight blueblack hair, gray at the temples, and an amiable calm about him, as if he were a favorite uncle. A gentle, disarming smile greeted her above his trimmed, shiny beard, and she found herself trusting him. He did not look dangerous at all.

"Wiley Smart, livestock proprietor, at your service, madam. A fair deal for everyone, is my motto."

"Why, yes, I'm Hannah Holt."

"I'm pleased to do you the favor of supplying shelter. Hospitality is a Smart trademark, copyright, and patent," he said. "There will be no charge, of course, under the circumstances."

"Charge? I thought it was abandoned."

"Not at all. I am simply keeping a prudent distance away until these dratted troubles are over. I suppose you wouldn't like to add another fine draft animal to that noble mare of yours? I have magnificent beasts and harnesses to match, including wagon tongues and doubletrees to alter your buckboard."

"No, really —"

"It'd double your safety on the trail. Move faster in a pinch. And you'd not be helpless if an animal gives out . . . or takes an arrow — not that any infernal Sioux would aim arrows at so lovely a vision of female pulchritude as yourself, of course."

"I don't think —"

"Well, I didn't expect you to. It's how I make a living, and I will try all comers once, and no matter the result, I have made a friend. No one leaves unsatisfied from the Smart Road Ranch. Now, of course, I have a fine line of shinplasters, liniments, horseshoe nails, harnesses, buggy whips, bran, if your fine mare is having, eh, problems; surcingles, reins, hoof rasps, turpentine . . .”

“I don’t need — I couldn’t afford —”

“Why, of course not, Missus Holt. And it makes no difference. I’m simply inclined to ask everyone. You never know when you’ll make a sale and a friend. But I’m going to give you a gift, anyway. I normally charge four bits for stalling a horse and two bits a day for pasture, but you are such an estimable lady that I will let that pass and settle for less when the time comes, with my great compliments.”

“I thought this place was abandoned.” Then she puckered. “You are a dear man and I shall reward you.”

She pecked him on his black-bearded cheek.

“Now that’s a reward fit for a captain of industry,” he exclaimed. “If Wiley Smart may be of any further service . . . I’m yours, madam.”

“Miss. Miss Holt. I’m on my way to the arms of my intended.”

“Oh, oh, that is sad, glad.”

She was golden in the candlelight and knew what the yellow flame did to her complexion.

“The dear man is waiting for me in Saratoga Springs, New York, for the nuptials,” she said. “That’s why I am so eager and why I’ve braved the bloody Bozeman Road.” She gazed sweetly at him. “I have a proposition for you.”

"A proposition? A proposition?" He beamed beatifically. "I am all ears and all yours. At your service. Ready and willing to perform any deed, any deed at all, no matter what, of all sorts and descriptions, whether simple or complex, whether skilled and difficult, or something to be done by brute strength or force of, ah, manly will . . . I stand ready —"

"Oh, my, that's grand. You are a dear man. Yes. I shall reward you. I would like you as my escort to the Bridger Cutoff and a little beyond. Then I'd be out of harm's way. It's only a hundred miles or so, isn't it?"

Wiley Smart gibbered a moment. "More like a hundred and a quarter, perhaps two weeks with that buckboard. But no . . . no . . . I can't imagine doing that. No, indeed. Quite impossible. At least for anything less than, oh, a thousand dollars."

Hannah swiftly hid her disappointment. "Why, I was going to reward you handsomely. You're such a fine, strong bull of a man."

"Ah, no, not even bulls wish to be scalped. No, indeed."

"But you just said you'd perform any deed, climb any mountain . . . well, never mind. I was only asking. I must get through, and fast."

"I wish I could be of service, madam, but —"

"Miss."

"Miss Holt. I tell you what. In exchange for the free board I have provided your beautiful mare, you may cook me a breakfast of antelope."

"But I've already paid you, dear man."

"Paid me?"

"Why, yes. I don't just kiss any man, you know. Just those who are very dear to me, those I favor, loving friends."

"Well, let's have breakfast. It's still dark, and we can chance a small fire."

She peered through a crack in the shutters. "No, it's not. There's a streak of light across the east. I must be off, Mr., um, Wiley, before this place becomes a trap."

"It's too late. If there's light at all, it's too late, drat it. This is the prime time to attack."

There was a sharp thud at the door.

"What was that?" Hannah asked sharply.

"Blow out the candle and I'll tell you," Wiley replied.

She did, and he slid open the shutter a crack. A revolver had materialized from somewhere on his person and was in hand now. From the open window he peered around at the door.

"An arrow," he announced. "Hmmmm."

A muffled clop of horses came to them in the murky false dawn. Hannah was frightened to the bone. She ran for her Henry. Was this the end? Here on the Bloody Bozeman? With a quarter million dollars banked in New York? She wept, furious with herself. She should have pulled out when Linc did.

"What is it? Are they Sioux?"

Wiley listened and caught the faint sound of moving horses. He sighed. "No," he said. "Not Sioux. That's a Crow arrow."

"How do you know?"

"The fletching. The feathers. Each tribe has its own way of making arrows . . ."

"Then what — ?"

Wiley slammed the shutter shut. "That was Buffalo Tail. He's done it again. He's the best horse stealer they've got."

"Horse stealer?"

"Yes, indeed. The dratted Crows are the best horse thieves of all the plains tribes. Masters of equine aggrandizement. Doctors of scientific thievology. Professors of the swipe. Your little mare is gone, and so is my fine running horse, Chief Two Coups, named after my dear friend . . ."

Hannah was appalled. "But can't you do anything? I must have that horse! How do you know that this Buffalo —"

Wiley Smart sat heavily on the rawhide bed. "Buffalo Tail's a Crow headman. He's run off my horses eight or ten times, and then I've had to buy them back. I have to trade good saddles and wagons and racehorses for them. Except once I pawned off a lame mule, or, ah, that's not my usual way of dealing, of course, heh heh . . ."

"But the arrow!"

"That's his way of counting coup. His bit of knighthood knavery. Does it every time too. If I'd left the dratted arrows in, my door would look like a porcupine."

"But what am I going to do? Did he take my wagon?"

"Of course not. The Crows are allies of the whites."

"But now I'm helpless . . ."

"Of course not, madam. Never fear. I shall sell you another strong, brave harness horse of noble bearing and great heart. Or maybe I can negotiate with Buffalo Tail. It will cost, of course, something for Buffalo Tail and a little fee for my services . . ."

CHAPTER
FOUR

Dawn cracked the eastern skies, and Linc felt encouraged. He'd huddled on the banks of the Boulder River, angry clean through and waiting for light. Here he was, with only two cartridges left, no warm clothes, and crude moccasins that would wear out in a few miles. He had to get to Bozeman Pass and over it somehow.

He stood and stretched — and flattened himself on the moist grass. Upon rising, he had seen in the gray dawn four Injuns on horseback, and two unmounted horses. They'd kill him for sure. Well, he'd take two if he could. Didn't even have enough cartridges for the four . . .

But the Indians didn't see the boy in the lavendar light and passed thirty yards away, heading down the Boulder to the Yellowstone, the same direction Linc was going. He hugged the cold earth, feeling dew soak his shirt, his heart tripping, and stayed that way until long after the riders had vanished and the tawny sun popped over the eastern slopes.

He couldn't get to Bozeman now, with all them Injuns over there on the trail. He turned back to the road ranch. A faint plume of smoke rose from the chimney, and he supposed she had risked a fire. He wondered if that owner-man was still around. He circled first to the barn and found the mare gone, as well as that owner's horse. Maybe that was what the Injuns had. Maybe over at the cabin Hannah and that man were scalped and dead. But the loaded buckboard was there in the alley, and that puzzled him. Why hadn't the Injuns looted it?

The door of the cabin was open, and as he approached, he heard voices. Alive, then. And not very cautious, if this here was Red Cloud country and those Injuns had just stolen horses.

"The horses are gone," he said in the doorway.

"Oh, Linc! You gave me a start!"

Linc found himself staring into the black bore of a Navy Colt. The livestock trader had it out and aimed faster than Linc imagined was possible.

"Oh, it's you, kid. Don't you know enough to hail the house? I thought you were up the trail."

"Wild Injuns on the Yellowstone," Linc replied, "so I come back for a bit."

"Buffalo Tail, probably, and the horses he stole. Don't worry about him, kid, he's Crow."

"I want some breakfast," Linc said.

"I'll cook you some, and then you'll be on your way," said Hannah.

"Yesterday yuh were begging me to hang around. Now yuh can hardly wait to get rid of an orphan."

"You'll do fine in the goldfields, kid," Wiley said soothingly. "Miz Holt and I were just discussing the purchase of some fine draft horses from my select stock, and I have offered her a bargain price in her distress. Don't you know enough not to interrupt your elders?"

"All I want is some cartridges — .56 caliber — and some boots."

"Well, young pipsqueak, how will you pay for these costly accoutrements and paraphernalia? If you can pay, I shall offer you a square, fair deal. Fair deal for everyone, I say."

"I'll work a few days for yuh?"

"Work? What work? I have fled to my mountain eagle's nest and have no work for the duration."

"Well, what am I supposed to do? Die?"

Hannah interrupted. "Never you mind now, Linc. Here, eat this and we'll decide what to do." She handed him a tin plate burdened with broiled antelope, and he ate greedily.

"Now, as I was saying, Miz Holt, I have two fine gentle draft animals, sound of hoof and long of ear, and harnesses to match. And because of your great misfortune at the dratted hands of Buffalo Tail, I will offer them at half price, two hundred each, plus a hundred for the additional harness, and I'll throw in the wagon work for free, because I am a fair dealer and every sale makes me a friend."

Hannah stared at him, hands on hips.

"Don't do it," said Linc. "For one hundred dollars I'd steal your mare back from the Crows."

"Your counsel is not wanted, young man. Miz Holt is an intelligent, independent woman, able to heed her own counsel in distress and helplessness in the shadow

42

of the Oglala terror, and the massacres, and the bloodied scalps hanging from all too many a lodgepole. She needs strong, masculine comfort and support for a woman alone in a brutal wilderness — such as I happen to be able to provide. So indeed you may be off now, and there will be providence awaiting you in the Bozeman settlement or at Fort Ellis."

"Yuh got her over the barrel 'cause she needs a horse now. I figure you and this Buffalo Tail are in cahoots."

"Oh, ho, that's a good one!" exclaimed Wiley. "Buffalo Tail is an ancient and miserable provocateur and the agent of much distress on the Bozeman Trail."

"I bet he sells you what he stole," continued Linc stubbornly.

"You have a scandalous mind, young man, and now you may depart. But I warn you, with a tongue like that your worldly prospects are gloomy."

Hannah said, "I simply haven't the means, Mr. Smart. I'm just a poor but virtuous girl in distress . . . Might you consider credit?"

"Well, now, I can't possibly offer credit — people go down the trail, you know, so I never see or hear from them. But I'm always open to arrangements, and I deal. No one leaves Wiley Smart unsatisfied or friendless."

"Except orphans," Linc said. "Miss Holt, if this here Crow has the horses, for fifty dollars I'll go get the horses and give yuh yours back."

She stared.

"Impossible," said Wiley.

"No, it ain't, Miss Holt. I'll catch up with Buffalo Tail, and I'll trade him my carbine for the two horses.

Them Injuns all want guns. Then I'll bring your mare back and keep the other. And with the fifty dollars I'll get me another gun in Bozeman settlement, and have a horse too."

"Done," said Hannah. "Fifty dollars is very expensive and I barely have it, but if you can do it, Linc, in two days, I'll pay you for the mare. But I can't wait more than two days."

Wiley Smart cleared his throat authoritatively. "Now let's not be hasty, young man. If you entered Buffalo Tail's camp, he'd end up just taking your carbine. Then where would you be?"

"I thought the Crows are friends of the whites."

"Their friendship's a bit peculiar," Wiley replied.

Hannah said, "Linc, you're the best chance I've got. I'll fix you a bait of antelope and give you some Henry cartridges, too, for the bargaining."

"Ridiculous!" Wiley rumbled. "Buffalo Tail's twenty miles from here by now."

"That's for Linc to find out," she replied quietly. "Mr. Smart, I thank you for your generous offer, and of course we are friends. I am perfectly satisfied and will take you up on your kind offer to let me board here free."

"Well, now, that was just for one night — ah, yes, Miz Holt, I'll just stay right here and protect you while you wait."

"I thought you would be safer in the foothills," she replied. "I wouldn't want to cause a scandal . . . But of course you may come and visit me."

She shepherded the man and boy to the door and shut it behind them. They heard the bolt drop.

Linc stood in the sunlight, blinking, getting accustomed to this high plains morning after the gloom of the cabin. It was clear and warming fast. Wiley Smart stood beside him pensively.

"My mountain lair is fifteen miles distant, or near it. My livestock may be miles beyond that, and I shall have to do it shanks' mare," he muttered. "Drat the luck. I shall have words with Buffalo Tail. And as for you, lad, forget it. Get along now, straight to Bozeman, and don't come back to pester us."

"With two cartridges and these things on my feet?"

"Be grateful you're alive," intoned the man.

"I'm going after the horses."

"One of which is mine. If you keep it, I'll put the law on you."

"Then get it yourself," Linc retorted. "If I bargain for it, I'll keep it."

Hannah was beside herself. The mare was gone. She would have to pay through the nose for another draft horse, or she could put stock in Linc's dubious plans, or she could abandon the wagon and all her goods and start walking. Her feet hurt at the thought of it. She had no proper boots.

Maybe . . . she could leave the wagon here, walk back to Bozeman or Fort Ellis, and buy a horse and ride it back here. No matter what, she'd be stuck for days. It would take the boy days to find Buffalo Tail. It would take days for Mr. Smart to hike to his mountain refuge and bring some horses back. Or days if she walked clear over the Bozeman Pass. She peered out of the unshuttered window and cursed the sun.

Her funds were in New York now, but she had brought ten double eagles and had sewn them into a pouch she wore in her skirts. Two hundred in gold with which to purchase rail fare from the U.P. railhead in Wyoming to the east and to buy a few amenities and rooms en route. There wasn't money to spend on Wiley Smart's costly drays. She'd work on him, that's what she'd do. She'd get his prices down with a few smiles and promises, or even a kiss or two. She'd done it before. But now she'd let them both go after horses, and one or the other would succeed — always assuming, of course, that Red Cloud didn't show up.

The very thought chilled her. She thought of opening the door, inviting the man and boy to stay. But that wouldn't make it any safer than it was. Maybe less so.

Then she remembered she'd forgotten to give Linc the cartridges! She flung the door open and saw him standing near the barn, looking undecided and lost.

"Linc," she called. "I forgot to give you some cartridges."

The youth shuffled over. "Here," she said, dropping ten into his hand. "They are for my Henry. Do they fit your carbine?"

They didn't. His carbine was a .56 caliber Spencer.

"Well, take them, anyway — to trade with," she said.

The boy looked disappointed. "All I got is two shots," he muttered.

46

"Good luck," she said kindly. "You're a nice young boy to do this for a poor helpless woman."

"Helpless like a horned buffalo cow," he muttered. "Yuh ain't welcome. I'm doing it for myself, to get fifty dollars and a horse."

She smiled. "Of course, you might not get it if Mr. Wiley — Mr. Smart — gets back to sell me one first."

"Yuh'll deserve what yuh get and what yuh pay," he said tartly, eyeing the distant, diminishing figure of the muscular man trudging south up the Boulder.

"I'll be here, and whichever of my knights in shining armor rescues me, I'll reward him."

"With what?"

"With kisses."

"I don't want that stuff."

"You'll get what you want at Bozeman. May the best man win."

Then she closed the door again, as much to preclude any more sass from the boy as to rescue her privacy. She wished to bathe and would have to settle for some sort of spitbath.

She wouldn't let either of these males see how helpless she felt. Of the two, she was more comfortable with Wiley Smart. She understood the road rancher, knew what to expect. The boy was different. Every time he opened his mouth, something terrible burped out that she had to gloss over and pretend was never said.

She started a small, hot, smokeless fire to heat some water and began to skin out of her dress and her petticoats. She admired herself, as she always did. Her figure was her fortune and would rescue her once again when Wiley returned. It always did, whenever she saw a male with that look in his eye. That's the way it had been in Virginia City, and it didn't matter whether the man was a down-at-the-heels miner or a tough teamster or a great mining magnate in a brocade vest stuffed with Cuban cigars. They were all alike.

When she had arrived, she was poor and virtuous. Now she was rich and even more virtuous. She had resisted so many advances, she was sure she was even more virginal than previously. She had learned to preserve it by telling men things. About her intended, who didn't exist. Or about her late father, who actually wasn't dead; he had merely become an opium addict and was useless to her. She had simply pretended not to know him on the streets of Virginia City.

She had found a proper boardinghouse for a virtuous young lady, of which there were only a few in all of Virginia City. She had told Mrs. Moriarty she would wait there a few days for her intended. It was always best to seem attached. There was even a stuffed chair in her room with doilies on the arms; a chamber pot under the high bed with the corn-shuck mattress, and a washstand of oak with a beveled glass tilting mirror where she could do her hair. It was the mirror that decided her on the place, and Mrs. Moriarty's studied indifference to her boarders. She hated to be spied upon. She had, after advancing her rent, twenty dollars left; enough for a month if she starved herself. But she had no intention of doing anything of the kind.

She began to attend the new Episcopal Church because the Episcopalians were more worldly than the

48

Baptists, the other congregation in the mining camp. After a few church suppers and prayer meetings she had a coterie of admiring swain, mostly married. To these she had privately imparted her sad story — she had come to this rude mining camp at the request of her intended, but he was not here; some rumors suggested he'd died of consumption . . . and now she was nearly penniless and facing certain horrors as the only way to survive . . . unless, of course, some shining knight would rescue a girl in distress.

A knight did. A pale, jowly, bald old man married to a dried-up prune. A man with unbridled fantasies, to be exact. He loaned her enough to purchase a narrow board-and-batt commercial building on the lower edge of town. She in turn rented it to a saloon keeper for a quarter of his gross.

In one month she was out of the boardinghouse and in her own cottage. In three months she had hired a crew to build her another commercial building on a lot a swain had given her as an earnest token of his undying love. He was an Irish miner named Burke, with a fine tenor voice and a poke full of gold. She had kissed him and smiled sweetly and promised much more when she had let him hug her once, briefly. At that very moment she had sighed and confessed to him that she didn't miss her intended as much as she had at first.

And so it went. The lots in town had come to her in various ways, mostly masculine. She'd acquired two of them by backing a busted faro dealer who won them at his tables. Within another year she had moved to a fine brick house above town and hired domestics. In every circumstance, save one, it had been her association with males that had paid off for her. The exception was her quarter-of-the-profits arrangement with Madame Marie Antoinette, which was conducted in deepest secrecy without books and only in cash.

But she had never been happy. Virginia City perched upon the slopes of bleak sagebrush-covered hills, barren and desolate. Alder Gulch was a brush-filled bottom where placer miners scooped and shoveled and rocked and mucked to extract gold dust in the sands of the creek. On the horizon were ranges of snowy mountains with the promise of trees and water and verdant meadows. But they were distant, the promise illusory.

Hannah had loathed the place and its barbaric frontiersmen, its roistering saloons, greedy entrepreneurs, barbaric new rich who lacked even the rudiments of education or the refinements she cherished. These were people to be used, not cultivated, and when she had used them up, she'd go back to civilization and warmth before the cruel western sun and Arctic air ruined the creamy, smooth skin of her face and neck . . .

She frowned, annoyed by the faint sunburn that now tinted her young skin. She washed hastily, vaguely irked by this delay, this whole trip, this frustration at the brink of a new life.

There was a sharp thud at the door.

"Just a moment," she grumbled. "Linc, is that you?"

Silence.

She finished dressing except for the high-top shoes and opened the door a crack. It was bright out and she blinked. The high plains sunlight was ferocious in that clear air. She saw no one. She opened the door farther to peer about, and then saw the arrow embedded in it. She started involuntarily. It seemed identical to the one that Wiley Smart had pulled from the plank, but she wasn't sure. Indians. The realization seeped through her body like a wave of ice, and her heart tripped.

Still, there was no one.

"Linc," she called. "Are you there?"

But it wasn't Lincoln who seemed to materialize but a tall bronze man, nearly naked, wearing only a breechclout and fine, fitted summer moccasins. His hair hung in two braids, and except for an eagle feather in his hair, he had no other adornment. She glanced aside, embarrassed by his nakedness, and then, against her wishes, stared. He was a fine figure of a man, lean and muscular, with a wide, coppery chest, narrow hips, and powerful legs. But it was the Indian's face that drew her at last; liquid brown eyes staring at her, promising a keen intelligence. High, prominent cheekbones, a beaked nose, an aura of dignity and authority. And in his hand a sinew-wrapped bow with another arrow nocked and ready.

And beyond him, three others stood, similarly dressed, all young, all menacing, all armed with Henrys.

Her heart raced. Who were they? Crow?

"Yes?" she said weakly.

"I am Buffalo Tail," he said with a curious slurred accent. "Absaroka — what you call the Crow. I have found your horse and will trade it to you — maybe. If you have anything to trade."

CHAPTER
FIVE

Wiley Smart had no friends and didn't really want them. Over the years he had grown independent and self-sufficient and accustomed to living alone.

Now, as he trudged southward up the shallow valley of the Boulder, his mind was not on his misfortune of being unhorsed but on how he might profit from the unexpected visit of a female pilgrim long after the trail had been shut down.

His feet hurt. He was walking in high-heeled riding boots not intended for long overland hikes. But it didn't matter. He would do what he had to — in this case, walk to his refuge in the foothills. He did not hike down the center of the valley, where he might easily be observed from the terraced hills to either side, but hugged the western edge of the bottoms, where he would pass less visibly. Even though his mind was on other things, his eyes and senses were alive to the prospect of trouble, searching horizons, wind, the silence, for anything out of the ordinary.

He was a hard man, without fat. The frontier and his chosen profession had kept him lean. And he was lightning fast, not only with a revolver but also with ropes and reins.

He had come to manhood in the hills of western Kentucky in the 1850s, at a time when the secession fever was strong among some neighbors, while others were equally determined to remain loyal to the Union. He ignored all that and instead took to horse trading, which came as naturally to him as breathing. He had found an abandoned homestead there and made it a base where stock could graze. But mostly he was an itinerant, with six or eight animals on his string, making trades from hamlet to hamlet. And during these youthful journeys he had mastered the art of amiability, looking directly at others with frank hazel eyes; speaking gently; praising his prey; confessing some innocuous weakness or other in disarming fashion; discovering that timing was a key to sales; discovering what buyers really wanted — beauty, utility, dash, soundness.

It has been an act. The direct gaze, words, and gestures that signaled honesty and trust, the tone of voice that bespoke truth — these were all mastered as coldly as a rifleman masters marksmanship. What little there was of Wiley Smart vanished, and the chameleon was born. Wiley Smart never noticed the change.

He knew all the tricks and invented a few himself. He picked up saddle-galled animals that owners had abandoned as hopeless and trained them to harness and a new life. He could conceal cracked hoofs, make lame animals walk normally at least until the sale was consummated, file horse teeth to remove the telltale signs of age. But above all he could talk with a calculated patter that directed the buyer's attention to the things he wanted the buyer to see.

He thought that was how others lived and scarcely realized that his little world was without tenderness or affection or trust, or that he esteemed no one, least of all himself. He supposed the whole world was populated with knaves and fools.

When the Civil War loomed, he chose neither north nor south but west. He started up the Oregon Trail with a small string of good, marketable animals, and along the way he discovered others that had escaped or been abandoned. Some were permanently lamed and useless. Others had recovered from trail ailments, and these he added to his string, which followed behind his big gelding on a long picket line.

By the time the rush started to the Montana goldfields at Bannock and Virginia City and Last Chance Gulch, he saw opportunity rising and followed along. At the place where the Bozeman Trail reached the Yellowstone and branched toward Bozeman and Bridger Passes, he saw his chance. Here was a protected valley rich with pasture; a natural resting place, and far enough west so that the pilgrims would arrive with footsore, exhausted oxen; lamed horses; gaunted animals.

They came almost daily during the migration months, and if they didn't have cash he accepted other valuables, especially furniture — cherry-wood tables, oak dressers and bedsteads, walnut chairs and commodes. These treasures he periodically hauled to the gold camps where furniture was scarce, and made an additional killing.

All this he did alone, with no hired hands whatsoever. He didn't trust them. He offered none of the amenities of the usual road ranch; no saloon or other entertainments. Not even shelter. He didn't want people lingering; he wanted them gone and far away before they got to reconsidering their transactions. He often called himself Colonel — a name that had a certain cachet among horsemen, and always he wore a black frock coat and brocade vest and other accoutrements of a man of substance. These garments combined with his steady gaze to make pilgrims feel instinctively that they were in good hands. He salted that impression with a collection of biblical quotations; he had a fine stock of them for every occasion, duly employed whenever a buyer or seller wavered, as a kind of ultimate authority, or sanction, for the trade. That was the extent of his religion.

By late afternoon, Wiley reached the junction of the Boulder and East Boulder Rivers, and here he wearily forded the river, soaking his pants, and headed southeast into an exquisite sheltered valley with dense cottonwoods along the creek, along with willows and aspen brush, and beyond, verdant meadows, now tawny. To the south towered the Absaroka Mountains, and to the north rose a great hump of prairie, a spin-off of the mountains, which deflected the north winds and made the spot an ideal one for wintering stock.

He had built a dugout into a hillside, along with a small corral, all concealed by aspens along the creek.

He had also built several caches where he hid reserves of everything that might otherwise be looted by the thieving Crows or other tribes. It was relatively safe here because it was off the beaten path, though still vulnerable to the Indian hunting parties that were after the teeming deer and elk in the valley. He kept his stock close at hand with a salt lick and natural barriers.

As he trudged wearily up this side valley he encountered some of his horses and mules and oxen, but he lacked a catch rope or bridle, so he had to walk the final mile to his hideaway. His feet had blistered, but he had never been a quitter. It gave him a sense of safety to be here; with luck he might ride out the Red Cloud troubles.

He dragged himself into his dugout at last and began tugging the boots off his swollen feet. It was a comfortable place with a sod roof, a back wall of native rock, log walls, and a puncheon floor. He was more comfortable here than at the road ranch.

As he doctored his blistered feet his mind focused on the author of his current troubles. Buffalo Tail, the Crow headman. The subchief had stolen a horse or two every few weeks as a sort of tax upon Wiley for building the road ranch on Crow land. Nothing had ever been said or negotiated. The Crow had not taken Wiley's other goods. On the rare occasions when Wiley had first resisted, firing on the horse thieves, Buffalo Tail had merely doubled his next theft as a lesson, always counting coup with an iron-tipped arrow in the door. When Buffalo Tail showed up occasionally to trade for Wiley's small stock of goods — cartridges or sugar or coffee beans or iron arrow points — he always, with a faintly mocking smile, paid Wiley with a stolen horse. And he was always accompanied by three or four young warriors just in case the loner, Wiley, might cause trouble.

But this raid was different. Buffalo Tail had also taken Wiley's saddle from the barn — with its sheathed saddle carbine and its kit tied behind the cantle. In the kit were pemmican, jerky, cartridges, and a slicker of canvas impregnated with India rubber. They had plundered Hannah Holt's wagon, too, but he did not know what had been taken. Perhaps nothing at all.

Colonel Wiley Smart had no doubt what it all meant. The Crows, encouraged by Red Cloud's wars of extermination, were on the brink of joining their ancient Sioux enemies against the whites, and the old alliance between Crow and white was on the brink of collapse. With the slightest provocation Buffalo Tail might capture all three of them — Hannah, the boy, and himself — and trade them to Red Cloud for torture or slavery or worse.

Lincoln Larrimer struck the Yellowstone and trudged west along its south bank, looking for Crow Indians and finding none. He was no tracker, but there were horse tracks aplenty on the bank of the river. After hiking several miles west, he reversed himself, gimped back to the junction of the Boulder, and soaked his feet there. The river water was cold.

He was in a melancholy mood. He had found no Indians to trade with, and he was determined to get to

58

Virginia City. For a moment a black rage swept through him. He remembered the war party that had caught his family. They were painted for war — black and carmine streaks on their cheeks and arms. He knew that much, that Injuns on hunting trips or traveling peacefully didn't paint up. But those were, and he knew they were Sioux as he listened to the howls and cries of his mother and father, listened while he pressed his small body hard into the hollow of earth. When it was silent again, he had cautiously peered through the sagebrush, thinking they had left but they hadn't. There, where the Bozeman Road looped around the northern flank of the Big Horns, he watched in sick dread as the big Studebaker wagon with bows on top was looted, the dray horses slaughtered by men the color of shining gold. When he saw one lift a scalp of his mother's long caramel locks, and then his father's brown hair, Linc could look no more and pushed his face into the dry dirt until the seizures of his stomach caused him to vomit what little was left in it. He wanted to stand up and walk down the long, shallow slope and shoot his carbine until he himself was killed. But he didn't. He clawed the earth with his hands and stayed still. What had saved him was that he was lying in a place with no obvious cover at all, the tiniest depression on a featureless sage-covered grade.

He remembered it all again as he had remembered many times in the month since it had happened. And with each memory searing his young mind, his fear, rage, and deadly hatred toward all Indians deepened. He was not inclined toward self-pity but toward murderous rage. If he couldn't bargain with this Buffalo Tail, he would attempt to steal a horse, even if it took his last two cartridges.

But first he had to find that thieving Crow. He looked longingly up the Boulder River Valley where the road ranch lay but trudged instead eastward along the majestic valley of the Yellowstone. The rimrock was gray here, not yellow, and the broad valley was warm in the sun.

For a mile more he hiked east, until he knew his raw feet would carry him no farther. The crude moccasins were little help, and beneath the thin leather he felt every pebble and stick and sharp-edged stone. Even grasses and roots seemed to pierce his soles. There was no sign of recent passage here, no fresh horse apples, nothing but a benign silence and the lazy circling of ravens. He had little choice but to return, and to save further wear on his aching feet, he climbed the south slopes to angle across open meadow in a line that he calculated would drop him down in the Boulder Valley about where the road ranch stood.

He'd rest his feet and try again! He'd go out every day to find them. Maybe he'd go on east down the trail a bit and find where those Crows all lived.

His calculations were good, and as he topped a long roll of prairie he could see down into the Boulder Valley. There were long, green coulees creasing the prairie as it dipped steeply toward the bottomlands. Far to the west, the river glinted silver wherever it peeked coyly from the cottonwood and brush along its banks.

A little to the south lay the small black forms of the road ranch.

He slipped into a wide coulee, knowing enough not to skyline himself. But for the darkness and anger in him, it would have been a glorious afternoon.

Another few hundred yards brought with it a growing awareness that something was different about the ranch. There seemed to be people — small, dark dots. One was Miss Holt; he could see that, even at a distance of half a mile. And he spotted a horse, a roan, pinkish at this distance.

"Injuns!" he exclaimed aloud. "That's Injuns!" A fine terror swept through him at the very thought. Now he was paralyzed. He wanted to flee. But Miss Holt seemed to be sitting quietly in the grass outside the cabin, her skirts spread out. The others were squatting near her, doing something or other.

He had to get over to the next coulee south and follow it down if he hoped to get close and see anything. Fearfully he altered his course, paralleling the Boulder, crouching low and gliding slow and small over the open prairie. No one below seemed to notice. As far as Linc could tell, the Indians had their back to him.

In the next coulee he slithered downslope rapidly, a little gnome of a person darting closer to the strange gathering below. Then he could see them all clearly. Miss Holt and three red men in breechclouts or leggings sitting next to her. Something flashed gold. Squinting, he saw Miss Holt drop the shiny things before one Indian, maybe the headman, with braided hair and an eagle feather. Was it gold? Was she paying him a bunch of double eagles for her horse?

He squirmed a little closer to another thicket of sage, and then he saw what it was. She was using those Henry cartridges to bargain with. She was paying them bullets to get her horse back. He couldn't make out how many, but it didn't seem to be a whole lot. Just a little pile.

Then he studied the Indians. Big ones, the color of red clay, all grown-up men, and hefting Henry repeaters whose brass glinted and flashed in the sun. Well, no wonder they wanted those cartridges. The Injuns were always short of them, and that heap would kill a bunch of buffalo — or a bunch of white men. He shuddered.

But where were the horses? There were three big Injuns and Hannah, but not a horse in sight. That baffled Linc. In the dawn murk he'd seen four riders go by. There were four then, three now. Well, maybe one was holding the horses off somewhere out of rifle shot of the cabin. That's how they did it, those Injuns. There had to be a horse holder somewhere. But where? He studied the open country and found nothing. Likely in the river brush, he concluded.

Then one of the Injuns led the roan mare over to Miss Holt, and she took it. And seeing that, Linc realized that he'd been cheated out of the fifty dollars Hannah had promised him if he got her horse back. It enraged him that Buffalo Tail had brazenly dickered with her for the horse he stole. And she had paid him up! Now he'd never get to Bozeman or the goldfields!

He stared at his battered carbine, his torn and elbowless shirt, his shredded britches, and a cold rage rose in him. She'd betrayed him. Maybe he'd just kill those Injuns and grab a horse . . .

He knew what he'd do. He'd steal one of the Injun ponies, maybe two, from that horse holder and maybe scatter the others so they'd be delayed in chasing him.

He crab-walked through the sage to the next coulee south, which debouched into the river flats south of the barn. There was a copse of aspen there and no direct line of sight to the cabin. There he saw some shadowy forms of horses deep in shade. And then, as Linc peered through the canopy of green aspen leaves, he spotted the slim figure of an Injun holding four saddled horses. A fifth unsaddled one cropped grass nearby. Smart's horse, Linc figured.

Linc silently slithered down the remaining slope to the aspens. The Crow horse holder seemed to be staring toward the barn rather than toward the slope behind him. He was a boy, a youth no older than Linc himself. Linc studied the horses, picking the one he wanted. Then, coldly and unafraid, he leveled his carbine, drew the hammer back, and stalked to point-blank range twenty feet away. When a horse wheeled nervously, the boy turned.

Their eyes locked. The Injun stared at the leveled gun.

"Gimme them horses," Linc said, pointing with his carbine.

CHAPTER
SIX

She trembled. So intently had she stared at them that she scarcely realized one was holding her roan mare with a hackamore rope of braided leather.

She smiled weakly, her body still trembling. "But that's my horse," she said.

"Now it is not," Buffalo Tail replied. "You are alone, yes?"

"Why . . . just for a moment. My intended —"

"What is 'intended'?"

"The one I shall marry."

"Where is he? Not Wiley Smart the trader. Not the boy."

She was caught in her lie. "Uh, he's coming soon."

Buffalo Tail stared. "He is lucky. You are very pretty —"

She lifted her head proudly.

"— but too pale. Like a spirit. Maybe not good in the robes, either. Trappers say the Crow women are better . . . I learned your words from the trappers. From Jim Beck-wourth. They wintered in our lodges."

She froze. The language unglued her. But then she relaxed. He was like any other male, she suddenly

64

realized. And she could use that. And here, indeed, was her roan mare . . .

"I'm sorry," she said brightly. "You're such nice men, and I have not made you welcome. I'm glad you're here."

"No, you're not," Buffalo Tail replied. "You're shaking inside like an aspen leaf, and you would slam the door on us but for this mare of mine. You have not asked, but I will introduce you to my young hunters. This is Thunder-in-the-belly and Many-women-laughing."

She nodded and stepped outside.

"Sit here," Buffalo Tail said, pointing to some grass near the cabin. She did. The Indians did likewise, forming a small circle.

"Where are the other — where are your horses?" she asked timidly.

"My son holds them. Horned Moon. You are passing through Absaroka lands, your horse ate grass, and this Bozeman Road scares away the deer and elk."

"I didn't know it was yours."

"Of course you didn't. You whites never think of what the Absaroka people — or other Indians — possess. Do you have anything to trade? We have looked in your wagon."

"I'm very poor —" she began.

"No, you are rich. Your dresses have many fine stitches and are made of thick cloth. You pay white dressmaker with needle many suns of work."

"But — I have only a little money."

"Money, gold. What is that to Absaroka? Think of what else. If we took your money to a trader, he would say we stole it. Wealth is war horses and buffalo runners and repeating rifles and buffalo robes and cartridges and —"

"I have a few cartridges," she said, suddenly animated. Actually she had six boxes of fifty each, minus those in the magazine and what she had given to Linc.

"I have the .44-caliber rimfire for your Henrys — but only a few."

"For this fat mare we want three boxes, one box for each of us."

She was beginning to enjoy this. "The mare is not worth it. I can buy another for much less. Ten. I'll give you ten cartridges each, take it or leave it. The mare's not worth any more."

"If you want this fat mare, three boxes."

"Wiley Smart has lots of horses."

Buffalo Tail nodded slightly to the others. "We thought so. He is afraid of the Oglala and has gone to his hiding place. He thinks he is safe there, like a rabbit sitting on top of a coyote den."

"He's bringing me horses to trade right now."

"If you buy horses from the trader, we will steal them from you. If you buy this fat roan mare, we will not steal it from you. Two boxes — that is the price."

That gave her pause, and also an idea.

"Two boxes are too many for a little old horse. But you are very nice Indians, and I do like nice Indians, so if you would like to escort me to the Bridger Road and

66

down it a way, until I am safe, I will give you two boxes."

He threw his head up. "The Bridger Road goes through the heart of Absaroka. Why do you think you'd be safe there? The Absaroka people are the best horse thieves of all."

"Because the Crows — always — they're friends of ours."

"Not always. Blanket Chief Bridger was not always a friend of the Absaroka." He paused, and there was a chill in the air. "Do you want to know why he is called Blanket Chief among the Absaroka?"

Her heart tripped. "I don't think I —"

"Blanket Chief took a Flathead for wife, but there are many Absaroka children who look like him."

She frowned. "Don't be fresh with me, Mr. Tail. I've heard about you Crows."

"What have you heard?"

The other Crows were laughing softly. "I shan't repeat it. You're a gentleman, and I only trade with gentlemen."

"I am no gentleman. I am red savage and you a white lady."

She didn't like this turn of conversation. "We were talking about a hundred cartridges and your escort."

Buffalo Tail frowned and stared toward the mountains. "No. It is not worth it to tangle with the Sioux. Red Cloud closed the Bozeman Road. Now I close the Bridger Road."

"Then I will go back the way I came. I don't need your mare and I won't trade cartridges."

"All right. We will go."

They rose and stretched. She let them. She would buy from Wiley Smart, and he would make a better escort.

"Twenty cartridges apiece — sixty — and we will leave you here with your roan mare."

"I will do it," she said. She raced into the cabin and dug out two boxes from her trunk. The three were seated once again, waiting solemnly. She counted out the twenties until there was a shining pile of brass before each one.

"Now I will take the horse," she said. "She's mine!"

"Not yet. Now we will talk about what you owe for going through our land, and eating our grass, and scaring away our game."

"But we agreed — all right, then. Keep the mare. I'm done trading." With trembling hands she gathered up the cartridges she had doled out and began fitting them back into the boxes.

He stared at her as she retrieved the shells.

"Perhaps we will take them, anyway," he said.

"You will not! The deal's off!" she retorted.

He nodded. Thunder-in-the-belly yanked the half-filled boxes out of her hands and raked the rest of the brass from the dirt.

"Leave my mare and get out of here!" she raged. She jumped to her feet and grabbed the lead rope of the mare.

In the next moments three things happened in rapid succession. First a cry rose from beyond the log barn. Then came the crack of a long gun of some sort. Then, moments later, horses emerged from the trees, clattering north. On the first, a brown paint pony, sat Lincoln Larrimer, and on a picket line behind him were three more ponies.

At this sight the three Crow warriors leapt to their feet. With practiced ease Thunder-in-the-belly grabbed the lead rope from Hannah's hands, slid over her back, and kicked the startled dray into a lumbering lope. In one hand was his Henry, and in the other the braided rope.

Buffalo Tail and Many-women-laughing raced toward the copse of aspen along the east bluffs. Hannah, paralyzed and suddenly horseless again, dragged behind, dreading what the Crows might find.

Off to the north, Thunder-in-the-belly was gaining on Linc, who was slowed by his picket line. At the last moment Linc released the horses he was towing and kicked his spotted pony into a flat gallop and pulled ahead. Or so it seemed for a moment. But even as Hannah watched, she saw the distant Indian slide off the mare, catch one of his fine Crow war ponies, and race after Linc with wild abandon. It would only be a matter of time.

In the aspen grove a youth about Linc's age lay on his back, a gaping red hole over his heart, staring sightlessly at the quivering leaves above. Buffalo Tail gazed bitterly at his lifeless son, and then both of the Crows knelt beside the still figure, muttering in a soft tongue she didn't understand. They lifted the dead boy and found his back, and the ground beneath, red with blood.

Buffalo Tail lifted the boy and carried the body toward the road ranch with Many-women-laughing trailing respectfully behind. Outside the cabin, Buffalo Tail laid the youth gently on the grass, and only then did he turn to Hannah with eyes as cold as Montana winter.

"Was that the man you will marry?"

Hannah cringed. The words slapped at her soul and belly like whips.

"He is a boy. He was hiding here when I came. I never met him before. His mother and father were killed by Red Cloud a few days ago. He . . . wanted to go west, to the mining camps."

Buffalo Tail waited stonily, but she was done.

"Into the cabin," he said. "But first hand me your rifle."

"What rifle? I —"

"The Henry for your bullets. The rifle you had when the bluecoats left you at the bend of the Yellowstone."

All feeling drained out of her. "You watched me from there?"

"We always watch the white man's road."

She slumped.

"Bring me the rifle. Then go into the house," he repeated harshly.

She thought wildly of pulling out her little revolver and killing him. Or herself. The Henry was there, glinting, powerful, protective. She well knew how to use it, but she could not bring herself to do so. In seconds she had seen her hopes and strength drain away, and now she was a dishrag.

70

She lifted the heavy weapon — had it always weighed so much? — and carried it, barrel up, to the door. Buffalo Tail grabbed it harshly, his eyes filled with grief. Beyond him, Many-women-laughing had arranged the boy's limbs, crossed his arms, and had begun a low, guttural chant that scraped against Hannah's nerves.

Softly now, from the north, rose the sound of unshod horses, a complex rhythm. Linc, on the paint, came first, sitting defiantly. Behind him was Thunder-in-the-belly, on a buckskin, his Henry boring steadily into Linc's back. Linc's battered carbine was in the saddle sheath. And behind him, the other ponies and the roan mare.

Buffalo Tail stalked close to Linc, staring at the boy. "You have killed Horned Moon, my son," he said.

Linc glared back. His answer stunned Hannah.

"When yuh steal horses, yuh sometimes get killed," the boy snapped. "When yuh go out on stealin' raids against other Injuns, they kill yuh if they can." Then he hawked and spat at the Crow headman.

Buffalo Tail froze, absorbing all that, and then, almost casually, batted Linc clean off the pony.

It knocked the wind out of Linc. He curled on the grass, gulping air like a small wild animal. Then he grew calm, and his eyes riveted on Buffalo Tail, who stood motionless over his son.

Linc sprang like a catapult, skinning knife in hand, and lunged at the headman. "Hooah," said Thunder-in-the-belly with a grunt. Buffalo Tail whirled too late, arcing his bow. It deflected Linc only a little, and the skinning knife slashed along the headman's ribs, not cutting deeply but raising blood that started to sheet down his left side.

Thunder-in-the-belly smashed the stock of his Henry across Linc's back and shoulder, sending the boy sprawling into the grass, and the skinning knife flying. The boy collapsed in wild pain, sobbing.

Hannah watched in horror. The boy gasped on the ground, blood in his nostrils, a wild thing. Buffalo Tail dropped his bow and hugged his rib cage, reacting suddenly to the sharp sting. Linc tried to get up, the wildness in him ready to fight to the death. Thunder-in-the-belly lifted his Henry and shot. A deliberate miss. The lead smacked into the soft earth inches from the boy's face and brought sudden, frozen fear into his eyes.

"Yuh killed my ma and pa," he wheezed. "Now yuh can kill me, or I'll kill yuh all."

Many-women-laughing grunted and lashed Linc's wrists with a thong. Buffalo Tail was hunched up, clutching his chest.

"I'll help you," she said wildly, almost beside herself in fear and confusion. "I have something."

She fled to the cabin and found a clean cotton shirtwaist, which she brought to the headman. With a fierce yank she tore it into a long, wide strip and bound Buffalo Tail's chest tightly with it. Over the wound the cotton crimsoned rapidly. She tore another strip and tied it as tight as she could over the first, and the red stained through that too.

72

Buffalo Tail gazed woodenly at the boy, who seemed to have only rage and no fear at all in him as he lay bound in the grass.

Hannah watched him, too, but without sympathy, for it had occurred to her that this twelve-year-old Lincoln Larrimer had dashed all her hopes, had used bad judgment, and might yet cost her her life or force her into a terrible degradation.

Suddenly she felt like killing him, which horrified her. She had never before entertained a murderous thought. But now she was aware of something forbidding about herself.

"I am sorry," she said to Buffalo Tail. "I never met that boy until I got here."

The headman said nothing.

"I hope you won't hold this against me."

His response was withering. "He is a brave boy and one I understand. He is a better white man than you. You are a coward."

Hannah recoiled. "Well!" she exclaimed, and found she had nothing to say. Did these Indians know only savagery?

They spoke among themselves in Absaroka, and she understood none of it. Their eyes were upon the distant aspen grove. Buffalo Tail stalked into the cabin, and when he emerged, he was carrying a blanket.

"But that's mine," she protested.

Disgust etched his face, and she lowered her eyes.

"It will bury the dead," he said.

Many-women-laughing untied Lincoln's ankles, prodded the boy ahead of him, and signaled for

Hannah to follow as well. Buffalo Tail gently picked up Horned Moon and carried the limp form toward the aspen.

Then, with trade hatchets, the Crows began constructing a scaffold of slender limbs, lashed with thong about seven feet aboveground. It took a while. The hatchets were poor tools with which to hack living tree limbs, but in an hour they had readied the burial place.

Buffalo Tail lifted the inert youth onto the red-and-black blanket and then added a few small things taken from Horned Moon's pony — a bow, a quiver of arrows, a small soapstone totem. Then the blanket was gently folded over the boy and lashed tightly. Buffalo Tail carried his son to the platform and laid him there, grunting from the pain it caused him.

The Crows seated themselves and began a strange and discordant chant. To Hannah it seemed to take forever. Linc sat down sullenly.

Then the Crows were done. Silently they prodded Linc and Hannah back to the cabin and pushed them inside.

She turned her back on Linc, who sat sullenly on the rawhide bed. From the little window she watched the three Crows build a small fire and drop boulders into it. Then they built an odd framework of willow poles from the river. Over this they draped the blankets from their ponies, as well as the canvas from her tent — which they had taken from her buckboard — until they had a serviceable sweat lodge. They rolled the hot boulders from the fire into it, cut sage and fresh

74

grasses, and then all three pulled off their moccasins, leggings, and loincloths and entered the lodge.

Hannah turned away and then peered back again, fascinated. Steam billowed from the place, and she caught the scent of sage and heard the low chant of Absaroka voices in prayer to the spirits.

It was strange but not frightening. There was a cleansing and purifying sense about it. She almost wished she could join them, but then she thought of their nakedness.

Their Henrys lay just outside the sweat lodge, and at times she saw one or another peer out through the cracks in the blankets and canvas. But apparently, neither she nor Linc had any thought of escape.

She turned to Linc. "Go wash yourself," she said sharply. "You smell and you're disgusting. I don't want you around me."

He seemed defiant.

"I wish they had killed you," she said bitterly. "You've ruined my life."

CHAPTER
SEVEN

Wiley Smart had a ferocious conscience but fortunately not a long-lasting one. The average duration of his pangs was about thirty seconds, and he had learned to wait them out, as he was doing now. In this case, the guilt had been with him almost a minute, which was most unusual and troubling in its own right.

Before him stood a bright red mare in blooming health. She seemed the epitome of fine horseflesh — muscled, calm, eager, sound . . . for the moment. He intended to sell her to Hannah Holt.

The mare had three normal hoofs, tan with faint, dark streaks running down from the coronet; a hard, tough horn. The fourth hoof, the offside rear one, was a different color, an odd, rosy, waxy, translucent tone. It was so soft and pliable that it sprang under the thumb. It also wore down with astonishing rapidity. But worst of all, it was so soft that the horseshoe nails worked loose a few days after a shoe had been tacked on. She had been several months now on the soft grass, pastured and waiting for the moment that Wiley Smart might pawn her off.

He debated whether to shoe her and decided against it. The shoe might be loose or off by the time he got her up to the road ranch. He'd take her barefoot, and if by any chance he couldn't unload her to Hannah, maybe he could trade her to that dolt of a boy for his carbine.

He knew, of course, that the mare would go ten or twenty or thirty miles down the Bozeman Road before going lame. He also knew that the lame animal could endanger Hannah's life during this time of Sioux warfare. And that perhaps is why his conscience squirmed overlong on this occasion. But he had not gotten where he was by heeding that siren song. Caveat emptor, that was his motto.

In truth, he found delicious pleasure in skinning anyone on a trade, and this one looked more delicious than most. He knew the type; it was not as if he were skinning some widowed immigrant woman. She was one of his own kind, skinning Virginia City of its gold even as he intended to skin her of some of her loot. He didn't for a moment believe she was as poor as she let on.

There were good, sound draft horses out on pasture he might have traded her, but those he would keep against the time when the Bozeman Road reopened to pilgrims. He would write a bill of sale, and it would say the mare was sold as is, no refunds. Truly a keen horse trader made more money than a horse breeder.

He debated taking a second dray to sell her as well but decided against it. It would mean converting her buckboard to take a team, bolting on a tongue and doubletree.

He haltered the red mare and saddled a long dun with a dorsal stripe. He added a good Winchester carbine with a saddle ring in the stock that allowed him to hang it from his saddle horn with thong. In his kit he placed several boxes of cartridges, some jerky, a canteen, and his spyglass. With the Sioux around he had to be extra careful. Leading the mare, he pushed his horses up the great hump of prairie to the north, and when he had reached the ridge, he hid the animals in a ponderosa grove and began to study the sweep of land with the glass, concentrating on the far reaches of the east where the lordly Sioux might lurk. He didn't rush; his life depended on his care. For half an hour he glassed the Yellowstone Valley and the rough, rolling prairie to either side but found nothing.

Satisfied, Wiley Smart cut north with his trade mare toward the distant speck of his road ranch. The mare was docile behind him, walking easily on a hoof that had grown out on soft pasture. Some hours later Wiley glassed the road ranch once again. There was nothing stirring, all quiet, except for Hannah Holt's pinkish roan mare tied to the cabin post.

"Drat and damn!" exclaimed the trader aloud. That infernal boy had bargained for the roan mare, after all. No doubt the Holt woman had paid the little punk a pile of shinplasters to seal her part of the bargain. And no doubt, double drat the luck, the varmint was right now riding toward Bozeman on Wiley's gelding, also recovered from Buffalo Tail. That varmint had more moxie than a badger in a hole. Wiley stewed a while. Here he was, the slickest horse trader in the territory, and the mark had gotten her horse back. Well, maybe she'd buy another for security. Getting past Red Cloud was a powerful incentive to buy, and two drays were better than one. That was it! He'd sell Hannah the bright red mare, anyway! He slapped the spyglass shut and dropped it in his kit, glad he'd caught up with the woman before she'd hightailed out.

It was preternaturally quiet in the road-ranch yard as Wiley rode in. His gelding twisted its head from the roan mare, which whinnied suddenly, toward the barn. As he rode past the cavernous, dark doorway a shot jolted him. It struck his saddle horn with a smack, spraying tiny bits of fiery lead into his hands and face. The thong holding his Winchester was neatly severed, and the carbine slid to the manure.

At the same instant Buffalo Tail and two warriors, all painted, appeared in the barn doorway, Henrys leveled on Wiley. The startled horse trader had only an instant to wonder why the Crows were painted, and then realized the white stripes were the mourning color rather than the black of war.

Buffalo Tail hailed him solemnly. "Slippery Tongue! You have returned to your nest."

"Shhh," hissed Wiley. "I am greatly honored by the fine Absaroka name you have bestowed on me in jest, and for which I am bonded to the People of the Raven. But, my friend, it is a name just between us Indians, eh? Among the whites I'd prefer you call me by my Christian name, Colonel Wiley Smart, or, of course, Professor or Doctor, for indeed I am the child of a pious and sober family."

Buffalo Tail's gaze was affectionate. He peered closely at the red mare, his eye settling at last on the hind hoof.

"Put that thing up," said Wiley. "Let us parley. What is than roan mare tied to the cabin? What has happened here? We shall have a smoke of the peace pipe, and I will tell you of ways to profit."

Buffalo Tail nodded at Many-women-laughing, who trotted out and collected Wiley's Winchester from the manure.

"All right, then, Colonel — or Professor — Smart. Tell us how to profit."

Wiley was relieved. He slid off his dun gelding, glad that the black barrels were, for the moment, pointing elsewhere. He strode into the barn.

"So, Slippery Tongue, you are hiding in your dugout that you think the Absaroka people don't know about," said the headman. "Perhaps we will let you stay there. Perhaps I will tell the Sioux dogs about it."

Wiley coughed.

"We shall decide later. We are deciding now what to do with that woman and boy. We will probably torture and kill the boy. Maybe sell the woman."

"That varmint?" asked Wiley. "He no doubt deserves every bit of it. Do it slow and make it painful. What scoundrel thing has he done to you? Steal those horses? Where's mine, by the way, heh-heh."

Buffalo Tail shrugged. "Yours, white man? The boy killed my son. We have sent Horned Moon to the beyondland."

The news numbed Wiley. He glanced furtively at the three Indians, loosely fingering their Henrys, and decided to sit down with them.

"Harrumph," he began. "Yes, the boy deserves it. Yes, indeed. Finish the varmint off and do it slowly, I say, so he has time to think about what he's done. And, of course, sell the woman. Worthless. I might buy her myself for a bit or two."

Buffalo Tail disagreed. "He is a very brave boy. Almost like an Absaroka boy. Maybe I will torture him slow so he can show how brave he is to the Absaroka people. Maybe I'll spare him. Maybe I'll kill you instead. Some white man must pay for the death of Horned Moon."

"Well, hch, it was that woman with him. No doubt she planned it. Put the blame on the right party, I always say."

"We don't know what to do with the woman. Very beautiful. Like ice. Might fetch a good price; maybe the Flatheads would buy her. Maybe trade her to the dog Blackfeet for torture. They like to burn women alive, especially white women. Watch them scream and hear their flesh sizzle like a hump roast. Sell her to the Sioux so their squaws can cut her to bits with knives. But she has cold eyes and thinks like you. No Absaroka would ever take her."

"Yes, my friend, I agree. No self-respecting Absaroka would want her. Your fine son would be alive now if she hadn't —"

"Do not talk about my son."

Wiley lapsed into silence, but his mind was churning. Advantage was the unfailing remedy for all hot spots, all troubles. Always offer someone the advantage.

"Well, eh, Buffalo Tail, I have brought you a gift today. That fine red mare that I brought here is for you, my friend." He paused. "But I should expect, of course, a few modest favors."

The headman glanced at the mare. Then he spoke rapidly in the Crow tongue to the others, who had mastered less English from the trappers. English. It seemed to Wiley that they jabbered a long time. He felt the sweat at his armpits and on his breastbone. There was no sign of life from the cabin. It looked more and more to Wiley like he'd have to shoot his way out of this and then skedaddle from this country.

"You are a skunk," said Buffalo Tail. "Worse than a Blackfeet. You do not stand and fight for your helpless ones. A helpless woman. A boy with no mother or father. The Real People — all the tribes, even our enemies — the strong warriors think first of the helpless ones. You are a big skunk, good only for the smell."

Wiley no longer cared what the headman thought. His salvation lay with Colonel Colt. There was another long silence as the headman pondered.

"The white man's gold road is no more. Forever more this land is Indian land. The Sioux to the east; the Absaroka here. The travelers are no more. No more trading horses for you; no reason for you to be here. No reason for the Absaroka to let you stay and use our land. I have decided. We will take your animals —

horses, mules, oxen — that are in your little valley. And you will go. Maybe east into the land of Red Cloud. Maybe west into the gold camps. But not south down the trail of Blanket Chief Bridger, which is the center of Absaroka, the land of the Raven people. I am closing the Bridger Road too. Like Red Cloud."

Wiley sat very still.

"We will think more about the woman and the boy," added Buffalo Tail.

In one stroke the headman had stripped Wiley of all his worldly goods. It left him in a quandary. Unless he killed them . . .

But first he'd try friendship one last time. "From the earliest days of the beaver trappers," Wiley intoned, "the Crow people and the Long Knives and all white men have been friends. The whites have traded with you, traded for Henry rifles, cartridges, ball and powder, iron axes and arrowheads and pots — so that you have become strong against the Sioux and Blackfeet and Cheyenne, and have grown rich stealing their horses, and fat shooting the buffalo with Henry repeaters. Now do you want to throw all that away? Think again, Buffalo Tail, my old friend. Think of your people."

Buffalo Tail nodded. Then, slowly, he translated it for the Crow warriors.

"Times change," he said at last in English.

The cabin door opened and Linc emerged. Thunder-in-the-belly raised his rifle.

"I gotta go. If yuh got to shoot me, go ahead," Linc yelled sullenly and trudged toward the privy.

Buffalo Tail motioned, and Thunder-in-the-belly lowered the rifle.

Wiley sat in the grass with the cold knuckle of fear in his gut. Never before had his golden tongue failed him. But these Crows were different from white men; unfathomable; motivated by hoodoo; with goals Wiley didn't understand — and that left him soaked in anxiety.

He peered into the eyes of the headman and saw grief and indecision. Buffalo Tail didn't know what he intended to do, that was plain. The three Crows sat cross-legged on the grass near the barn, Henrys across their laps, consuming time. It maddened Wiley, this waste of time. Savages were time wasters, like children.

His mind was full of options. If they took his livestock, he'd be penniless, and it wasn't at all certain he could start up again with the sort of captive trade he enjoyed here.

"My bosom companions," he began mellifluously, "I have been considering my future as well as the future of my brothers the Crows. Now I'm thinking, after the Sioux quiet down and stop warring on Crows and whites, why, I'm thinking I'd like to turn this into a trading post for the benefit of my Crow brothers. Here I would offer the finest weapons: Henrys, Spencers, Winchesters, Remingtons, Sharps . . . ball and powder, cartridges, iron arrowheads, percussion caps, four-point blankets, cooking pots, axes, the finest horseflesh, and, of course, low prices for my favored customers — half price for the Crows, full price for outsiders. And I'd trade for fine buffalo robes, elk skins, other horse-flesh.

You set those lovely Crow ladies to tanning robes, and before you know it, every warrior will have his Henry to fight your enemies . . ."

Wiley beamed, but Buffalo Tail stared darkly, not answering.

Linc emerged from the privy and turned toward the Indians and Wiley rather than the cabin. He sat down sullenly beside Wiley.

"Go back to the cabin, boy," said Buffalo Tail.

"Yuh can't tell me what to do. If yuh are going to shoot me, go ahead."

A faint glint of amusement, perhaps appreciation, flickered across Buffalo Tail's face. "You will obey me, boy."

"I ain't a boy and I ain't gonna obey some savage."

"Now, Lincoln," intoned Wiley, "Mr. Buffalo Tail is a headman and deserving of respect and our kindest regards, a man most civilized and not savage —"

"I don't want tuh hear your fat lip," he said with a snarl, and stood up. "I'm gonna take that roan mare over there. The one yuh got from that woman — and I'm going tuh ride to Bozeman. Yuh got my gun, so I'll get even by taking the mare."

He stomped away. Something like respect glinted in Buffalo Tail's eyes, but then he lifted the Henry, aimed carefully, and shot. The bullet struck Hannah's mare just at the back of the skull and smashed its spinal cord. The mare trembled and then dropped.

"What did yuh do that for? That was the dumbest thing I ever seen. Yuh dumb Injun bastard!"

This pleased Wiley. With Hannah's mare dead, she had no choice but to bargain with him for the red mare or, he reminded himself, the Crows.

From the door of the cabin Hannah stared, horrified, at her mare, sprawled in a heap, its legs in the air, neck soaked in blood. Wiley watched her, smiling lazily to himself. He'd give her a few moments. She glared at Buffalo Tail, who had lowered the Henry to his lap, and stared at Linc, who fought back tears and stood helplessly, his fists clenching and unclenching.

She did not reenter the cabin. Instead she strode purposefully toward the circle of Crows on the grass, an amiable smile illuminating her face. Wiley realized with a start that she was all dolled up. Instead of plain trail clothes, she was decked out in a green velveteen dress. Her hair was combed and lustrous, tied back with a yellow ribbon.

"Mr. Buffalo Tail," she said sweetly. "I have prepared food for us all. Not much, I'm afraid. An antelope stew with some things from my airtights. And I have only three bowls, so we shall have to take turns. But do come. You and your nice gentlemen friends must be hungry."

Wiley couldn't help staring. The woman was stunning. It was a clean beauty that would appeal as much to a red man as to a white. Even as he watched, she was bewitching the headman with bright eyes, bright spirits, and a dimple to delight the angels. It was as if he had never shot the mare and destroyed her only means of escape.

"We will eat," said Buffalo Tail. He said something in Crow to the others and they rose.

When all their backs were turned to Wiley, he was tempted to pull out his hideout gun and shoot them. But he didn't. The consequences might be terrible. Instead he fell in beside Hannah.

"Ah, Miz Holt," he said mournfully, "they have indeed destroyed your lovely mare, that temple of eager horse spirit. But as it happens, I have brought with me here a fine red one, pastured yonder, that may be your blessed salvation. A splendid animal, a Minerva and Diana and Aphrodite of a horse, young and strong. And I will offer it at a bargain, too, disdaining to take advantage of your present distress. And, of course, in honor of your comely beauty. She's a fine mare, though, the finest I possess, and I must at least get my expenses out of her. But I forgo profit and gain. I shall sadly part with her for the small sum of two hundred cash, or cash and goods as necessary, and then you'll be on your way."

She stopped. "Colonel Smart," she said crisply, "I have no wish to bargain. I'm sure I can do much better dealing with Buffalo Tail."

CHAPTER
EIGHT

The Crow Indians ate quietly in the yard outside the cabin, and then Wiley, Hannah, and Linc ate as well. The boy seemed famished and cleaned the stew pot.

When the meal was done and Hannah was putting away bowls, Buffalo Tail stood at last and summoned them to the yard. She found herself staring again at the loinclothed headman, fascinated by his powerful, coppery body. It somehow unbalanced her, leaving her unsure of her powers over men.

"I have decided," Buffalo Tail announced. He waited calmly for that to sink home. "The Absaroka — you call Crow — have always been friends of the Long Knives. That is the way, and I will honor that even though the whites are not always friends of the Absaroka."

Wiley beamed, certain that his trading-post proposal had sunk home. He dabbed absently at a little splotch where the antelope stew had dribbled onto his gold brocade waistcoat.

"So the Absaroka will do you no harm, even though the boy has killed my son. I have listened to his words and they are true — those who steal horses can expect to die. The boy talks truth. He would make a good Absaroka boy."

"Yuh letting me go now?"

"No. I have decided something else. We do not want whites in the land of the Absaroka. This land is too good for the white man. We do not live only on the plains like the Lakota Sioux or only in the mountains like the Flatheads. We live in a land that has plains and mountains and rivers and buffalo."

Hannah wished the man would get on with it. Her fate was in his hands.

"I will not let you go south down the Blanket Chief Bridger Road through the middle of Absaroka. I will not send you west toward the mining camps. I will not send you north to Fort Benton and the fireboats. I will take you east to the ashes of Fort C. F. Smith, to the Lakota lands, and leave you there. And if Red Cloud lets you pass, you will be safe. And if not, the Sioux, and not the Absaroka, will be to blame."

That plan suited none of them.

"But —" protested Wiley.

Buffalo Tail raised a palm. "Be quiet. I am not done." He paused. "Do not pull your hidden revolver out, Slippery Tongue, or you will be full of holes."

"Yuh think I'm going east, you're crazy!" snapped Linc. "Yuh gotta kill me first."

Buffalo Tail looked benevolently at the boy and said, "You are blessed with a true tongue. But you will go with the others."

Hannah clenched and unclenched her fists. "You'll give us my buckboard and a draft horse, surely?"

"I will. Slippery Tongue brought a red mare to trade to you, and you will have that. And I will return your

Henry and ten cartridges so you can shoot meat. You will have what you need. Wagon, horse, gun."

"Yuh gonna give me some moccasins? I got nothing to walk on," the boy said.

Buffalo Tail muttered something to Many-women-laughing, who strode off to the barn where the Crows' gear lay.

"You will have a pair, and my own elk-skin shirt."

Wiley was stewing. The mare would go lame soon.

"Ah, Buffalo Tail, my old friend, my *amigo*, bosom brother. I had, ah, very special plans for that mare. Yes, indeed. That mare, that prize mare, was intended to be a gift — yes, indeed — a gift of honor to you. Yes, a thank-you for the honors you have done me. Keep her close. She has special medicine."

Something glinted in Buffalo Tail's eye.

"I am honored, Slippery Tongue."

"I thought you might be here and brought her all the way from my mountain hidey-hole for you."

Hannah looked quizzically at Wiley. Not an hour before, Wiley had been earnestly peddling it to her.

Buffalo Tail said, "And I in turn give it to this white lady to draw her wagon."

Wiley drew a kerchief and wiped his face. It was late in the day, and the September sun was low and cool, but he felt flushed.

"Well, eh, yes, very nice, very nice," Wiley muttered.

"Thank you, Mr. Buffalo Tail," Hannah said, beaming. "You're a dear man and I adore you."

Buffalo Tail frowned.

90

"My red brother and bosom friend," said Wiley, "with all of us in that wagon we really should have two drays. The mare and another. Yes. A tongue and a doubletree and two stout drays. Now I just happen to have a few more —"

"Be glad I am giving you a horse."

Many-women-laughing returned with the clothes and handed the items to Linc, who eagerly pulled his crude footgear off and slid his feet into a fine pair of high elk-skin moccasins.

"Hey, this is something," he said.

When he had pulled the elk-skin shirt on, he looked almost prosperous — and not a little Indian. He took care to keep the crude moccasins, which would be spares.

"Now I'm going to the camps. Yuh gotta kill me tuh stop me," he exclaimed. He had a full belly, his skinning knife, and clothing enough to make it.

The boy bolted toward the river and its trail, and was fifty yards gone before anyone reacted. Buffalo Tail nodded, this time to Thunder-in-the-belly, who broke into an easy Indian lope. He would wear down the boy soon.

"He has spirit like a good buffalo runner," said Buffalo Tail in English. "But he is too young to be alone. He will go with you."

Wiley fumed. He hoped the dratted boy would get loose. If Wiley had to go east with Hannah, he had certain designs, and the infernal boy would only be a nuisance. Let Buffalo Tail escort them to the ashes of C. F. Smith. Once the Crows were out of sight, he'd wheel that buckboard northwest toward Benton, rather than risk Red Cloud.

"Eh, Buffalo Tail, my noble headman friend. The more I think upon it, the more I'd prefer to drive those geldings of mine in your, eh, possession. The one I rode today and the one I had the other day. I do enjoy training the beasts. What I will do is leave you that fine red mare and we shall hitch the two saddle geldings. I like to do people little favors, and as I judge horseflesh, I judge you'll have much the better of it."

Buffalo Tail folded his arms. "No, Slippery Tongue, you shall have the red mare to pull your cart."

"Is that your Indian name, Slippery Tongue?" asked Hannah. "How did you ever get that?"

"Why, my dear Miz Holt, that is a boyhood name my mother gave me once when dosing me with castor oil, and somehow my dear friend here ferreted it out of me when I was in my cups — oh, yes, a weakness I confess to — and teases me with it."

Buffalo Tail leered. "Colonel Smart, my white friend, the mare is yours. But as a token of my undying esteem, I shall give you both geldings back. I'd hate to see you stalled even before leaving the land of Absaroka."

"Buffalo Tail, you are a noble chief, the greatest of all the Crows and then some, a demigod and Jupiter," cried Wiley. "We shall train the saddle geldings to harness, and that dratted boy can ride the red mare."

Hannah Holt listened to all of this with a certain puzzlement and then dawning recognition. She eyed Wiley the way she eyed beggars, hard-rock miners, and

92

curs. The big fraud — in his gold brocade vest, black frock coat, and scruffy, laced high tops — was a windbag, and it looked like she might be forced to travel with him. The only solace was that he seemed good with a gun.

She smiled affectionately. "Why, dear colonel, we shall have a very nice trip and good company. You are an amazing storyteller." She eyed Buffalo Tail cozily. "Now, if only I could persuade Mr. Tail to escort us safely down the Bridger cutoff, I would be most happy and most grateful. Why, Mr. Tail, I'd do just about anything to thank you."

The headman stared at her coldly.

Wiley said, "It's Buffalo Tail, not Tail, my dear woman."

She blushed prettily. "Oh, dear, I'm so sorry. Buffalo Tail, this twilight is lovely and the air is mild. I'd like you to escort me for a little walk, and perhaps we shall see the moon rise over the mountains."

"I prefer to ride horses," he replied.

"Well, walk with me to the river and keep guard while I bathe my feet. I wouldn't want Indians, ah, Red Cloud, to come while I have my shoes off."

In truth Hannah Holt was desperate. She didn't want to be taken deep into the land of the Lakota Sioux. The orphaned Linc was living evidence of what the Oglala and Hunkpapa and Minneconjou were capable of. She still had her buck-board and supplies. All she needed was a draft horse — and freedom.

There was one more arrow in her quiver, and though she detested the idea, it might be that or death. She would offer herself to Buffalo Tail — if he agreed beforehand to escort her on the Bridger cutoff to Fort Laramie. She slipped her arm into his.

The headman seemed willing enough, but before they had gotten a dozen steps from the cabin, Thunder-in-the-belly returned with Linc. The boy was in a rage, and his wrists were bound with thong.

The boy beelined straight toward Buffalo Tail. "Yuh think yuh can keep me, but yuh can't. First chance I get, I'll go to the gold camps like my ma and pa wanted."

"Not if we take your moccasins away," replied Buffalo Tail quietly.

That possibility subdued Lincoln. He skulked into the cabin and threw himself on the bunk.

Buffalo Tail turned soberly to Hannah. "I am in mourning. Four days I must mourn my son. That is the sacred number. I will tell Many-women-laughing to guard you while you bathe at the river."

"But Mr. Buffalo Tail —"

He turned away, some unfathomable disgust upon his face, and barked something in Crow at the stocky warrior. Many-women-laughing approached, ready to walk down to the Boulder, but Hannah rebelled. She whirled toward the cabin.

"My feet are fine," she muttered, trembling slightly and close to tears. The cabin was gloomy in the last twilight, and she could barely see Linc on the bunk. Some flicker of luminosity on his cheek told her that he had been crying.

Buffalo Tail stood in the twilight watching the last streak of blue light behind the Crazy Mountains to the northwest. For a moment his face softened into a reverence for the plains and mountains and the great river that spelled home for the Absaroka people. Then he turned toward Wiley.

"Our white brother will join the savages in the barn tonight," he said. "The woman and the boy will stay here. Before you join us, Colonel Smart, you will give us your hidden six-gun, and we will give it back to you when we leave you at the ashes of Fort C. F. Smith."

For a long moment Wiley didn't answer.

"Slowly and with the grips first."

Wiley peered slantwise. To one side Thunder-in-the-belly held a Henry at the ready. Wiley sighed. His trump had been overplayed. He eased his hand in and pulled it out. He might still flip the revolver — he had practiced endlessly — but some caution forbade it. He handed it to Buffalo Tail.

"You will use Horned Moon's robe," Buffalo Tail said, "and keep it." There was a tone in the last three words that suggested he was not impelled by generosity.

"Tomorrow," said the headman loudly enough to reach those in the road-ranch cabin, "we will take you east to the land beyond Absaroka."

Hannah heard his words and quaked.

It was dark now, and she wanted to curl up in her blanket. "Turn your back, Lincoln," she said.

There was no sound. She pulled her green velveteen dress off and folded it. The dress had been magic for her before, making men's eyes light up, making them stare at her hungrily. But it was as if Buffalo Tail hadn't noticed. Well, that's how savages were. They never noticed nice things, pretty things. She doffed one of her three petticoats as well, and then slid into her bedroll.

Never had she been so afraid, with her fate hinging on the whim of one savage. And there would be no help from that windbag and mountebank, or from that obnoxious boy. She still had her little four-shot revolver, a tiny thing, in her blanket, and no one knew about it, but that was all. Small comfort it would be in a wild land with the Sioux ready to take her life and rip her scalp right off. In her everyday petticoat she had sewn a deep pocket to hold it, and now she decided to carry it there.

There was something about Buffalo Tail she liked, though she couldn't put a name on it. What had she done, proposing that walk to the river? A flood of shame raced through her. She had been willing to throw everything away. And on a savage too. Had she lost her senses? Always her successes had come from promising much and giving nothing. The more she promised, the more she received. Diamonds, pokes of gold, lots in town, meals, comforts! But Buffalo Tail hadn't responded. All he had said was that he was grieving. What kind of savage excuse was that?

Hannah was miffed. Then she felt sorry for herself. How had she ever ended up out here? Her sot of a father had written a glowing letter, gold everywhere, boomtown, opportunity, high society — letter after letter until she came. He was a contemptible man, weak, a visionary, a man who had never supported his

96

family and finally drifted away from a loveless marriage. Not that Hannah liked her mother, with her nagging and petty cultivation and poetry. Hannah's sole wish for years had been to get out of that house, and when her father had finally sent the means, she did. And then she found an opium-ruined derelict in a barbarous frontier town.

Death lurked in the dark door, and in the dark window now. Why, this very night a party of Lakota could come here — the place was right on the Bozeman Road, after all — and slaughter those Crows and the rest of them.

Maybe, she thought, she should go back west, take Linc with her. Was Saratoga Springs so important? Wasn't her life more important?

She thought again of the dream that had animated her for two years. She saw herself in the new casino dressed in the frothiest frocks known to Paris, sitting at a green baize table with a glass of claret in hand, enjoying the attention and yearnings of a score of wealthy, debonair men. Great entrepreneurs, suave, shaved, talcumed, with clean fingernails nicely honed, witch hazel, and white-coated servants everywhere . . .

But what was all that? Would it make her happy? She was sure it would when she had started this trip. But now she wasn't so certain. Was it a mirage? Why did Buffalo Tail seem to be a real man — the only one she'd failed to captivate? And the Colonel — ha! What titles that popinjay collected! Wiley Smart had offered no help, sought only advantage, and had never heard of love or caring or tenderness or the frailty of women.

What did Buffalo Tail have that she didn't? That awful boy Lincoln had it too. She couldn't fathom what it was, and that annoyed her. Why could that savage look at her calmly and be so at home in the world, as if he belonged here? She didn't belong anywhere, and not even Saratoga Springs would be home. Why had he cared about the death of his son? All Indians did was kill each other. That's what Indian war and horse stealing was all about!

She was uneasy, and it wasn't just the possibility of the Sioux coming. It was as if there were ghosts and demons here. But tomorrow she'd ask Buffalo Tail to escort them west, not east. She'd have one ally: Linc Larrimer. Somehow, thinking about the boy comforted her.

CHAPTER
NINE

The news that greeted her at dawn was that Buffalo Tail
and his two Crows were gone. She had heard Linc
shouting something and Colonel Smart growling back,
and she bounded out of her blanket, into her wrapper,
and out the door.

The pair of them were at the barn. There was no
Crow in sight. In the pasture were three horses — the
big red mare and Wiley's dun and bay geldings. Her
Henry lay on the ground. Wiley was retrieving his
revolver, which had been placed beside the Henry.
Hannah's buckboard stood unmolested in the shadowed
barn alley.

"Plumb gone," Wiley said, gloating, but then he
thought better of it. "That red rascal has gone up to my
hideaway, and I'll bet dollars to doughnuts he's
gathering up my stock!" The idea appalled him. "Over
thirty horses! A dozen oxen! Mules!" He saw his
fortune drifting away and turned brick-colored. "Drat
and damn!" he muttered. "I am bereft. That prize was
worth more to him than packing us east."

"He left three nags, one for each of us. I'll just git
mine and git going," said Linc.

"Think again, little boy. They're mine, all of them."

"Yuh numskull, he left one for each of us!" Linc retorted. "I'm gonna git going." He trudged toward the pasture, but the click of a cocking hammer halted him.

"Get lost, sonny."

"Stop that!" Hannah cried. "Let the boy have his horse. He can get to the camps with it. He doesn't have anything else — they took his carbine."

"The horses are mine, but of course I'm always happy to trade. A fair deal for everyone, I always say," said Wiley, his revolver never wavering.

Hannah picked up her Henry, and the bore of Wiley's revolver swung briefly toward her. She checked the magazine. Ten shiny brass cartridges slid out, exactly as promised. The weapon was heavy in her hand, the sun glinting off its brass frame. She felt its power. She had given little thought to guns before, or what this lethal tube could do for her. She swung it back and forth, sighting down it with a growing sensation that she held her destiny in her grip. She slid the bore past Wiley, who flinched slightly as it arced by him.

"Careful where you point that," he growled.

Did she detect fear in his voice? Good! She knew then what she would do. If Wiley would not yield the red mare soon, and at a tolerable price, she'd take it at gunpoint. But she'd bargain first, and if that failed, she'd get her horse by whatever means were necessary.

"I'm going to start some breakfast," she said. "Why don't you and Linc check the bluffs for Sioux? Maybe Buffalo Tail knew something we don't."

She carried the Henry, which seemed alive and deadly in the crook of her arm, into the cabin and slipped into her blue gingham. From the window she saw that the man and the boy had heeded her advice and were climbing out of the valley to check for Indians. The antelope had gone bad, and she hated to feed those galoots from her airtights, but she went ahead, knowing she'd be free of them for good.

They returned a while later. Linc said, "There's nuthing. Guess I'm gonna live."

"You should thank God you're alive," Hannah rebuked.

"God ain't got any use for orphans," snapped Linc. "'Least, not as I can see. It's me alone."

Wiley filled the door frame. "Ah, a delicious repast fills the nostrils. A banquet for kings, by a lady of exquisite beauty and virtue," he said, slightly emphasizing the last word.

They ate quietly. Then Linc addressed Hannah. "Whyn't you lend me that Henry and I'll fetch yuh more game?"

"What's to prevent you from walking off with it to the gold camps?"

"'Cause I'm honest, is why," he blazed. "Yuh need the meat. And I got to carry a lot since I ain't got my carbine now, and this dumbhead won't let me have the horse Buffalo Tail left for me."

"Careful how you address your elders, little boy," said Wiley.

Hannah sighed. "Colonel Smart, I think you should give the boy the horse, and he will be safely on his way."

"Ah, my dear Miz Holt, my heart grieves for the orphaned and the homeless, and I'd help mightily if I could, and as my Christian conscience dictates. But I, too, am in dire distress, for I am sure the Crows have taken every beast I had."

"You don't know that for a fact," Hannah replied.

"But I do. I know my brother Buffalo Tail as well as I know myself."

"Am I gonna get yuh meat?"

"Yes," said Hannah. "I trust you, Linc." She handed the Henry to him, ignoring her misgivings. The boy was transparent.

"I won't fail yuh," he said, and bounded out.

"A foolish thing to do, madam. That rapscallion —"

"I will trust him!" cried Hannah sharply.

Wiley stared blandly, like a green frog on a lily. "Now that he has that Henry and I merely a miserable six-gun, what's to prevent him from stealing my geldings?"

The thought amused Hannah. She peered out, but Linc had gone toward the river brush, not the horse meadow.

"Linc doesn't think the way you do," she said cheerily

"In my business it doesn't pay to trust overly much. All manner of sharpers and mountebanks and odious sorts want to trade bad horseflesh for good. I grow weary of it and of course bear the burden of dealing fairly with the pilgrims, the families of the road. A fair deal, indeed, is a cross I bear."

Hannah glared at him. There he sat, ruddy and with jet-black hair, his brocaded vest and grimy frock coat, sanctimoniously insinuating he was something he wasn't.

"Speaking of that, what's wrong with the red mare?"

"Good heavens, madam, has that dratted Buffalo Tail been insinuating . . . do you suppose there's anything amiss with that noble red beast? Why, I'd trust her if my life depended on it."

She arched an eyebrow. "Well, you and Buffalo Tail were fobbing it off on each other . . . and you changed your tune in a hurry the moment it looked like your life might depend on her. Suddenly you wanted your geldings instead."

Wiley looked hurt. "Your accusations grieve me in my soul, madam. I am touched to the quick. A more wounded mortal you've never seen. Ah, the unfairness of it, the injustice of it . . . If it weren't a sentiment from such lovely and innocent lips, truly I'd take offense. Yes, great offense."

"I'll buy one of your saddle geldings," she said.

Wiley groaned and twitched. "Alas, madam, the geldings are not for sale. My fortunes now depend on them. But . . . yes, I must say it. There's a modest flaw in the mare. She has, I fear, a tendentious inflammation of the cervical ligatures, the result, ah, of frostbit lungs. But tendentious inflammation of the cervical is no great calamity with proper management."

"I prefer either of your saddle horses."

"Then, madam, you shall have to go without a horse."

Hannah fumed. "If I need to run from Red Cloud, I won't be able. You're threatening my life."

"Not at all. A noble animal. She will merely be a bit sore around the inflamed membrane."

"How much?"

"Why, I had intended to ask a fine, square price of two hundred, but because of the minor defect, I'll let her go — with some reluctance, you understand — for one ninety."

"Fifty dollars," said Hannah.

"Unthinkable."

"Fifty dollars will start you going again."

"One hundred and eighty, perhaps, if it's in gold."

"I don't have it. I'll walk with Linc back to the Bozeman settlement and start over. Between us we can carry many things, and we'll have a gun and meat."

Alarm glinted in his eye for the smallest second. "Well, perhaps we could make other arrangements. Some cash now, perhaps other forms of compensation."

"I'll walk, thank you," she retorted frostily.

A faint, guarded look of disappointment flickered across his face.

Let him stew, she thought. If all this failed, there were other means. Of course, she told herself, she wouldn't actually shoot Wiley. Or would she? Maybe she would if she had to. But only wound him. Whatever it took, she'd have her horse.

He sighed, moaned, and muttered to himself. Then he rose and paced back and forth, up and down. "It's madness and I'm a chump. A veritable chump and mark and gull. One hundred in gold."

"Done," she said. "Go get the mare and I will give you five double eagles."

"Well, now, I was just speaking theoretically. My actual price is —"

"Get that mare now."

"Excellent, excellent. A fair deal for all." He charged into the sunshine.

She pulled up her skirts. At the waist of her petticoat was sewn a small leather pouch that encased ten ounces of gold. She removed five, worried that she'd not have enough for later.

He tied the mare outside and accepted the gold Hannah dropped into his sausage-like fingers, biting one after the other to make sure the metal was properly soft. He bloated up with joy.

"Ah, yes — ah, now there's the matter of the pasturage owing on her, of course. I've had her for six months now, and I should say another double eagle would cover it. I can't let her go, of course, without the board bill being paid."

Hannah turned to ice. "Pasturage for your own horse?"

"Why, no, indeed, Miz Holt. The mare was left here to recover from minor ailments by a passing pilgrim who of course intended to pick her up again."

"Then you have no right to sell her."

"Ah, but I do. The good man, an elderly minister — that's a one-owner horse — he asked me to, and to forward the proceeds to him in Oregon. Heartbroken he was to let her go . . . Stood in the pasture petting her and weeping. So that's what I'll do — minus a modest commission, of course."

"I'll think about it. No, I won't. The deal's off. Give me my gold and the mare's yours."

"Now don't be hasty," bellowed Wiley. "A deal's a deal. The horse is yours, now and forever, amen."

Hannah was ready to pull her little ladies' revolver from her petticoat, but just then a shot echoed from the river brush. It startled them both. Hannah peered out. Off in the distance, Linc stood over the sprawled red mound of a deer. She trembled. She would wait to get her Henry back and use it on Wiley if she must.

"Linc has a deer. He'll need help dragging it here."

She left him sitting there and plunged across the fresh meadows, tawny now, feeling the clean air on her face. Everything was so clean here, away from that dirty road ranch.

"I got him with one shot!" Linc exclaimed. "Two-point muley."

"With one shot!" Hannah replied. Then she remembered something she had been taught by her swain. Shots carry far. Watch awhile before you go to game. She did now, suddenly, scanning the bluffs on both sides of the Boulder River.

Nothing.

"We must be more careful," she said. She grabbed a foreleg, and Linc the other, and they slid the animal across the golden grass. It was heavy work.

"I don't see that fake colonel here helping," Linc muttered.

"Oh, Linc, that reminds me. I need the Henry now."

He handed it to her reluctantly.

"Wish I could keep it to feed myself on the way to the gold camps," he said wistfully.

"I tell you what, Linc. You have meat here enough for two or three days before it goes bad. You take some. And I'll give you some airtights. And some beans. Some red beans. And some matches. You can open the airtights with your skinning knife and then keep them to cook your beans in."

"Yuh fixing to take pity on an orphan?"

"No, just repaying you for the meat."

He smiled faintly, and it was the first she'd ever seen. "I reckon I could get there on that. Not that anybody'd help me when I git there."

There was a loft pole projecting from the barn that seemed made for the purpose, so Linc and Hannah hoisted the buck on it, and Linc began to butcher. Wiley emerged from the cabin, frock coat flying.

"Well, Miz Holt, your gamble paid off," he proclaimed cheerily. "I never supposed it would."

"What gamble?" asked Linc.

"The Professor didn't think you'd return with my Henry," Hannah said dryly.

"That figures. If yuh had given it to him, yuh'd never seen it again."

"I carry the scourges and whips of hard men, as Christ carried the cross," said Wiley. "It is my lot in life."

"I'm gonna git outa here, soon as I have a quarter cut off for me and Miss Holt packs me some grub," Linc said quietly.

"I am crucified," said Wiley. "My hospitality scorned. Now, Miz Holt, about that matter of pasturage . . ."

"I'll pay you when I leave. Now where's my bill of sale?"

"Why, madam, coming right up. It shall issue forth on the tide of the day, when you pay the pasturage. And, of course, there's a dollar transfer fee, and the Territory collects a four-bit tax."

She laughed. "Thank you. I knew I could count on you. You're such a nice man, and thoughtful too." Cheerfully she pecked him on the cheek, feeling the bristle of the black beard on her lips.

Linc had gutted the buck and was yanking the hide down the carcass, cutting and ripping with youthful impatience. "Looks like this old buck ain't the only one getting skinned around here," he muttered.

"Ungrateful wretch," Wiley said.

"Lincoln, watch your tongue," said Hannah. "The Professor bargains hard but has my best interests at heart. Don't you, Wiley?" Her shining eyes were upon him.

He beamed. "I confess, Miz Holt, I have misgivings about that mare. I have parted with her too low. I am thinking of buying her back for the same price. I could get double for her at Bozeman."

"Jeez," said Linc.

"My heart rebels at my own foolishness. But I shall count it as a tithe and a charity and an oblation to God."

"Colonel, I tell you what. You harness her to my buckboard and I shall take a quick spin with her to see how she goes, with you beside me to instruct me, and then we'll discuss the rest of it further."

He began to dance. "I'll do just that." With an expert hand he bridled the stout mare, fitted the collar and hames, tightened the bellyband, adjusted the breeching, and backed her to the traces.

Meanwhile Hannah dragged her trunk from the cabin and hoisted it to the buckboard. She grinned. "I'll try her with my wagon loaded," she said. "How are you coming with the meat, Linc?" she asked.

She remembered something, found a burlap sack in the barn, dropped in some tins of food, poured several pounds of beans into it, and set it beside Linc.

"There," she said, "that'll get you west. Oh, wait a moment." She dug into her gear. "Here are some sulfur matches wrapped in oilcloth. Now you're set."

She popped into her padded seat and slapped the reins, not waiting for Wiley. The mare lurched ahead powerfully and into an easy trot that suggested the buckboard was weightless behind her. Hannah was pleased. Coyly she turned back, knowing that Wiley was apoplectic, and pulled the obedient mare to a halt near him. Something in the back of her mind still troubled her about this mare.

"I won't sell her back," she announced to Wiley.

"Well . . . ah, then we shall deal with the pasturage," he said.

She stalled a moment. Linc had cut a hindquarter and was wrapping it in another burlap sack. He carried it to the buckboard and laid it in the bed.

"That's about all yuh can take afore it spoils," he said.

She was ready then. Free at last! Her heart tripped with joy.

"My dear Colonel," she said sweetly. "Thank you for your hospitality, for rescuing a lady in distress. You deserve more than I can repay you. I've cooked several meals from my stores, and of course the fee for those is twenty dollars in gold. And as a little love offering I'm leaving you the remainder of the buck, shot with my Henry and bullet, after Linc takes what he needs."

"Why, madam, your chow could not possibly cost —" For a moment he seemed unhinged. "Wait a minute! There are other considerations and fees, my good lady . . . I say, wait!"

But she was gone. And if he followed on a saddle horse, she would use her Henry. She wheeled north, traversing the lane until she reached the relentless ruts of the Bozeman Trail.

Just as she turned a bend, past a copse of cottonwood, she saw them on the bluff. There were five in sight on their ponies, half naked, staring at her and beyond, toward the road ranch. Some wore one or two feathers in their braided hair. Others wore their hair loose and at shoulder length. Their flesh seemed more golden than the copper of the Crow, and their faces were wider. They were not Crow. They were Sioux.

CHAPTER
TEN

Later she had no inkling of her reasons for doing what she did. She had acted instinctively. When she first saw the Indians, she had been about to turn east on the Bozeman Road. For an instant she had been tempted to flee west. Instead, heart in mouth, she wheeled the buckboard straight up the east slope of the valley, directly toward them. She was going to Saratoga Springs, and nothing would stop her.

She checked her rifle. The Henry lay at her feet, loaded and ready. In the deep pocket in her petticoat lay the revolver. Her spare Henry cartridges were back in her trunk. She lamented that, but at least the magazine had the ten that Buffalo Tail had returned to her.

She glanced behind her from the hillside. Linc and Wiley had seen the Sioux now. Linc grabbed his burlap bag and was racing toward the river brush. The Colonel was running with surprising ease toward his pastured geldings.

As she approached the crest of the bluffs the five Indians watched, bemused. They saw now that she was female. She did not slow down but lashed the mare into a faster gait, a lumbering lope that was bringing sweat to her neck and withers. She wrapped the reins around the whipsocket, lifted the Henry, and levered in a cartridge. But none of the five responded, although their weapons — a battered repeater in the hands of the one who seemed to be their leader, and carbines and bows in the hands of the others — seemed to follow her progress casually. The ribbon that held her hair slipped loose, and now the auburn hair flowed lazily around her shoulders. She raced right past them, forcing one to kick his horse out of the ruts to escape the rattling buckboard. As she passed, she saw them all in glimpses, saw not death in their eyes but amusement. Her glance lingered on the one who was different, paler, maybe even gray-eyed, though she passed too fast to tell. Then she was free.

But behind her, the headman gestured laconically; two of them started off in an easy lope behind her, and the others raced toward the road ranch where Wiley was frantically trying to saddle an edgy gelding that was spooked by Wiley's fears. And Linc had vanished.

Those behind her seemed in no hurry to close the gap. She glanced back in terror but saw no lifted rifle or pointed arrow. One of her pursuers was the more lightly colored Indian, who was probably a half-breed. She knew what she'd do. She'd run another mile or two and shoot them. The thought left her breathless. She'd never shot anything, much less from a careening buckboard. But she could let the mare run; it ran steadily so Hannah could concentrate on her targets.

She ran that mile and then another, and the big mare was winded. Her pursuers loped easily, just out of rifle range. Then the mare went lame. At first it was an arrhythmic gait; then a favoring of the off hind, and, half a mile farther, a lurching limp and a sickening slowness. She yanked the reins, whirled up the Henry, shot, and levered in another cartridge. She missed.

"No," shouted one of the Indians in English. She shot again, this time at the other, and it must have come close; the Sioux jerked his head and lifted a hand to his hair.

The lighter one was upon her then, leaned far to his left, and grabbed the Henry from Hannah's grasp with a jolt that pulled her arms half out of their sockets.

He wheeled his pony, grinning. "*La* mare, she makes lame, eh?"

It wasn't English exactly, something closer to French. This Sioux knew French! She was too shattered to talk. Was this the end? Or would this lead to the Fate Worse Than Death? She capitalized it in her mind, her way of underlining terror. The other Sioux was beside her now, his bow drawn, his arrow never wavering from her chest. It choked her throat to see it.

The mare trembled in her harness. The sweat had turned to foam, and the insides of her thighs were white with it. Easily the lighter Indian slid off his pony and lifted the mare's hind leg. The horn of the hoof was mashed and split and so splayed out that the mare had been running on the frog of her hoof.

He laughed. "Bad hoof," he said. "*La* mare, she is useless." He dropped the bad hoof and examined the others. "These make better. *Beaucoup* . . . ver' hard. You got bad mare, eh?"

She lost her terror long enough to fume. So that was Wiley Smart's little game and the reason why Buffalo Tail was laughing! She wouldn't have gotten far, anyway — Indians or not. A hundred dollars for this! And her safety and maybe her life too! That mountebank had cared so little about her that . . . that . . .

"*Très bien.* You are beautiful when you are upset." He smiled lazily.

Something sagged deep within her. She was probably a dead woman. So young. And so rich. If only she'd heeded them all and gone down through Idaho Territory to the Oregon Trail . . . The wonder is that the savages hadn't yet killed her. Did it mean they would torture and torment her or do . . . other things? She was comforted for a moment by the bit of dark steel in her skirts.

"Who are you?" she asked dully. She noticed now that he was not young, graying at the temples.

"Lame Cheval — Lame Horse. Also Charles Roque. *Ma mère*, Mother, she is Hunkpapa, like these my *frères*. Papa, he was a French trapper of the castor . . . beaver. He is *mort*. We are Hunkpapa Lakota!"

The Hunkpapa! One of the bands most closely allied to Red Cloud. Her heart froze.

"What," she asked timidly, "are you doing here?"

"Stealing horses from the Crow dogs."

"Aren't . . . you far away from your people?"

114

"Yes, far. Hunkpapa live near Paha Sapa, the sacred place of the Lakota many suns to the east. But we always war on the Crow. We will take many ponies, eh? But not this mare *rouge*."

He undid the harness and shoved the limping mare away. "*Au revoir*," he said to it, grinning.

He tied a braided rawhide rope to the singletree and dragged the wagon around.

"Where are you taking me?"

"To the others, to the river."

"Where did you learn to speak English?"

"At trading posts. Fort Union. We learn the words. Learn word for whiskey." He laughed.

The other Sioux tied a line to the buckboard as well, and they began to drag the wagon, and Hannah, behind them. It was still early morning, and Hannah supposed it would be the longest — or shortest — day of her life. She sat on the seat and wept as the wagon creaked back down into the valley. They had left her harness lying out on the prairie.

"Don't you want to take the harness too?" she asked.

He shrugged. "*Pourquoi?*"

She sat bitterly on the seat, braking as they descended the slope. She'd kill herself, that's what. But before she did, she'd kill Wiley Smart. If she died, so would he! She'd make sure of it. And if they tortured him, as the Sioux often did, she'd stand there and enjoy it!

The vision pleased her for a moment, but then she remembered Linc and dreaded the thought of what they might do to that luckless boy. Not that she cared

115

one way or the other now. If the boy had had brains and come with her, he could have shot both pursuers while she drove and escaped . . . with the red mare.

The trip down the slope and to the ranch lane took a long time. The ponies weren't used to pulling and didn't like it. And Lame Horse and the other Hunkpapa found that the dragging was tiring on their arms and rested frequently. As they rounded a bend in a long draw, she could see down into the Boulder Valley where the three other Sioux were holding Wiley Smart, his wrists bound, his two geldings nearby. But Linc was not in sight. Maybe . . .

"How come you to have zat mare *rouge?*" asked Lame Horse.

"That man there — he forced me to take her," she said bitterly. "I hope you torture him first so I can see it."

He laughed easily. "He trades the horses?"

"Yes. But the Crows stole all he had, almost."

He laughed again. "He deserves it. Now we will steal them from the Crows."

They dragged the buckboard to the vicinity of the barn and untied their lines. Even as the wagon slid to a stop, the other Hunkpapa began to paw through its contents, finding little to pleasure them at first. But then they found the remaining boxes of shiny brass cartridges and exclaimed happily.

Hannah's spirits sank again. What little she had was no longer hers. She felt the dread of a condemned man walking up a gallows stair and wondered if God heard prayers or even cared.

116

Wiley Smart sat in the tawny grass, his arms bound behind him and his frock coat askew. She glared at him, the author of her troubles.

"If that confounded boy hadn't shot that buck, we wouldn't have drawn these damnable savages down on us," he said with a snarl.

He did not notice Lame Horse's stare.

"Dratted boy has killed us all."

"Be quiet," Hannah hissed.

But it was done. The half-breed said something in Lakota to the headman, and with an easy gesture the leader sent three of his warriors into a wide search, two toward the riverbottoms and one toward the barn and the aspen copse beyond.

"He understood," snapped Hannah.

"Serves the dratted boy right if they find him. All his fault," Wiley retorted.

"I would have made it but for that mare. Shot them with my Henry and kept on going," she said. "You killed me with that mare and I hope you roast in hell for it."

The gray-eyed half-breed was listening, but she didn't care.

Wiley assumed the most dignified pose he could manage under the circumstances. "Miz Holt, that was my finest stock, especially selected with your needs in mind. What possibly went wrong with her? A pulled tendon? You were reckless with the whip, perhaps?"

She did not deign to answer.

"A deal's a deal," he added. "'A fair deal for all' is my motto. Don't try to sell her back. I fear you have ruined her."

Lame Horse and the headman stared toward the river where the two warriors were systematically probing the brush and finding nothing.

The headman was in his thirties, perhaps. Maybe forty. She caught herself staring at him, drawn by some shadowy charisma she couldn't explain. His broad cheekbones were so wide, they gave his alert face a diamond shape. His lips were pulled down into a permanent scowl. The nose was amazing in its length and width. It had the sharpness of an ax. And above it were deep frown lines etched on his forehead. His eyes glinted like obsidian marbles and were heavily bagged. And all of this on a powerful, tall, stocky body that showed no sign of age. He seemed at once holy and bloody. He glanced at her, and the venom in his eyes made her quail. He was the most frightening male she had ever encountered, and she felt as helpless as a moth in a hawk's beak.

"He is *le grand* Hunkpapa," said Lame Horse, who had caught her staring. "Ees medicine man, chief of all chiefs."

She stared at the earth.

"He hate ze whites."

That she already knew.

"He is called Tatanka Iyotaka . . . Sitting Bull."

The name did not mean anything to her, but apparently it did to Wiley, who shrank into himself. But then he seemed to muster something of his aplomb. "It is an honor to meet the great Hunkpapa chief and medicine man," he said, grinning lopsidedly, his eyes yellow with fear.

Lame Horse's eyes rested on the bulky trader and turned away. Sitting Bull did not ask for a translation.

Hannah noticed that a revolver was tucked into Sitting Bull's belt, and she guessed it had been taken from Wiley. When would they find hers? she wondered.

Her shining Henry was being fondled by Lame Horse. Sitting Bull grunted something, and Lame Horse promptly filled the magazine and trotted toward his pony.

"Always ze Crows to look out for," he said to Hannah. "We are deep in ze Crow lands to get horses if ze Crows don' get us."

With that he laughed and rode toward a bluff where he would do sentry duty.

Sitting Bull stared darkly at her, appraising her for the first time, his face inscrutable. His eyes lingered on her figure, and she felt both dread and opportunity in the gaze. Men were all alike. This Sitting Bull would be no different. But his eyes lingered no longer and settled upon Wiley Smart, reading the trader with practiced ease.

"Don't know whether you savvy English, my good man. But if you do, let me tell you about myself. Wiley Smart. At your service. I'm here to help the Sioux, help the Lakota. Yes, indeed. The despicable Crow have temporarily made off with my fine war-horses and buffalo runners, but I have more, many more. Yes, indeed. I'll mount the Sioux on the best horses in the universe, for phenomenal low prices, lots of credit, pay later . . ."

Sitting Bull's eyes turned away. There was no hint of understanding in them. At least not of the words. Down in the brush there was motion, and presently the warriors appeared. Ahead of them, raging mad, stomped Linc.

The boy kicked and snarled his way across the amber fields, his burlap bag arcing toward either warrior when he stepped too close. Linc was, nonetheless, a boy, and a boy's rage did not bother the men.

He stomped straight toward Sitting Bull.

"Well," he said, snarling, "yuh killed my ma and pa, and now yuh can kill me." He spat. Sitting Bull nodded, and a warrior hauled the kicking boy off to the grass near Wiley and bound his wrists.

"If yuh'd given me that gelding, I'd've got away," Linc snapped at Wiley.

Hannah thought it was quite probably true. Wiley had doomed Linc as well as herself. She was sorely tempted to shoot him. She decided she wouldn't. If she did, they would take her revolver, and she wanted it in case they started to torture her. And, anyway, maybe they would torture him too. He deserved it. Let him suffer all the way to hell.

Sitting Bull surveyed the road-ranch yard, the corrals and the buck-fenced pasture beyond. Then he approached Wiley, and his hands flashed a message in the sign language of the plains: Where are your horses?

Wiley had never mastered the sign talk and stared blankly. Sitting Bull realized that the road rancher's

120

hands were bound, and he untied them swiftly. Then he flashed his question again, but Wiley just shook his head. The Hunkpapa tried Linc, but the boy just stared sullenly. Then Sitting Bull muttered something to one of the warriors, who mounted his pony and rode up to Lame Horse's sentry post. In a few minutes Lame Horse returned to the ranch yard to translate.

"Where are ze horse of ze ranch?" he asked.

The question snapped the inert Wiley Smart to life like strings snapping a marionette. He rose, dusted off his frock coat, and seemed to expand like a watermelon. He found a stogie — his last — in his coat, and a lucifer, and, with practiced hand, swiped the lucifer across the shiny gabardine of the rear of his frock coat, lit his cigar, and puffed expansively, a transformed man. The change astonished Hannah.

He beamed. "You tell my fine new friend here, the Honorable Sitting Bull, chief of all Sioux, that I am Professor Wiley Smart, renowned for my advanced knowledge of equine life and disease . . ."

Lame Horse didn't get all that, but he conveyed what he could.

"Now, as it happens, the dratted Crows have made off with some — repeat, some — of my choice stock, but for a small consideration — a token, really — I am prepared to trade the rest; indeed, fleet and noble animals that can run down the wily buffalo, outrun any war-horse the Crow possess, and all as a below-wholesale bargain for my great new friend Sitting Bull and his fine Lakota . . ."

There was no shutting him up. Lame Horse struggled with a translation task that was quite beyond him. Then, with a simple authoritative wave, Sitting Bull silenced him. Wiley stopped mid-sentence, obedient to the strange force of the Sioux leader.

Lame Horse translated. "Sitting Bull says where are ze Crow? Where did they take ze horses?"

"Well you tell my fine *amigo* Sitting Bull that I have his best interests at heart. You tell him not to forget Professor and Colonel and Dr. Wiley Smart. For the smallest token of esteem I will gladly point the way taken by the dratted Crow thieves."

Lame Horse said, "Sitting Bull, he want answer, not wind."

"Well, yes. For some small guarantee I'll —"

Hannah spoke up quietly. "His horses were south of here, up the river. The Crow took them last night or this morning."

Lame Horse grinned and translated.

"Drat it, woman, now we're up the creek. I was negotiating for the safety of us all before you opened your sweet, ladylike mouth. For that I won't buy back the red mare."

Hannah laughed wildly.

"Sitting Bull say we go now to place up the creek and we will find the tracks of the horses and the Crow. You walk or die."

They stood uneasily while the Sioux mounted.

At the top of the eastern bluffs the red dray mare appeared and whinnied at the sight of the other ponies. She limped on down the Bozeman Road.

122

"I can't imagine what you did to her, madam. She was the noblest of my stock," said Wiley.

CHAPTER
ELEVEN

It was a long way, longer than Hannah had ever walked. They had not let her go to the cabin to put on more sturdy shoes. None of them had anything but the clothes on their backs. The September nights were cold, and Hannah wondered whether she would suffer without a blanket.

The walk would take the better part of a day, Wiley said. He had just done it, and his feet were already sore. Most maddening of all was Sitting Bull's refusal to let them ride the two geldings taken from Wiley. Sitting Bull led one; the other was ridden by one of the Hunkpapa warriors, who led his own pony. Hannah had worked her charms on Lame Horse and asked him whether she might ride, but Lame Horse had just shrugged.

"Walk or die. The horses are being kept fresh for war."

So Hannah walked. Easily enough at first but later with mounting weariness. And then the rubbing took its toll, and a crease in the leather of the left shoe pressed awkwardly into the side of the foot whenever the shoe flexed.

And behind, lumbering and limping along, came the lame red mare, whinnying gregariously to the horses ahead of her. It irked Sitting Bull. The noise was dangerous. But so might the rifle shot be that killed the mare.

At the end of two hours Hannah was desperate and ready to quit even if it was her doom. Only Linc seemed to weather the walking. His moccasins were the right size, and his feet were tough, anyway, from a barefoot youth. Wiley trudged ahead grimly, in obvious pain himself but showing an endurance that Hannah grudgingly admired. The Sioux were silent. One ranged ahead as a vedette. The others flanked the three prisoners and seemed faintly annoyed by their slowing gait. Or rather, Hannah's limping pace.

"Walk fast or you die," muttered Lame Horse.

"I don't care if I do or not," snapped Hannah.

By now each step she took was raw pain. But equally ominous, she was weary and her legs scarcely propelled her forward. She yearned to collapse on the grass. She begged God for a rest, a chance to sit on the riverbank and soak her bloody feet in the cold, soothing water. She had never prayed much, but now she offered God ten percent of her wealth if he would deliver her safely to Saratoga Springs — and soon.

Finally Sitting Bull halted.

Lame Horse approached Wiley. "How far now? Where are Crow?"

"Well, you tell my fine friend Sitting Bull that for a modest . . . ah, why, yes. We are a third of the way. Half a day more."

Hannah knew a half a day was impossible. Was this how it would end? A bloody-footed march, exhaustion so intense that it numbed her mind and blotted thought, and then a bullet or an arrow?

The Sioux were arguing among themselves. As she sat in the grass her spirits recovered a bit. This valley was transforming itself as they trudged south. Up at the road ranch the river had run between prairie bluffs. But now great spurs of mountains surrounded it, and rugged slopes, heavily forested, ran upward on both sides. The river itself coiled through verdant meadows, and along the stream were thick copses of cottonwood and aspen and willow brush. They had raised game frequently, deer and elk, but the pain in her legs had numbed her soul to the beauty and primitive luxury of this place.

Lame Horse came to her. "You ride lame mare. Other two walk."

She was surprised. It sounded cruel. The mare had gimped along behind them, gamely lurching to avoid putting weight on her sore hind hoof. But the mare was eager to return to pasture she knew and kept up. Lame Horse lifted Hannah onto the back of the lame mare, and Hannah pulled her skirts high to sit astride her. Colonel Smart stared at her legs. She grabbed a handful of mane and hung on, at once relieved and guilty.

From the back of the mare, life didn't look quite so bad. And Hannah could think again. Yes, she had lost her possessions. But if she could make it to Fort Laramie, with its telegraph, she could resupply herself.

126

And she was still alive, wasn't she? That was something. She was hungry — she hadn't eaten in a long time. She knew Linc was too. The boy was at an age when he had a hollow leg.

They started again. Linc, who had been sullen and silent, began to snarl. He stalked over to Sitting Bull. "Why don't yuh get it over with? If yuh don't kill me, I'm going to try for yuh anytime I can." The chief understood nothing but the tone. He smiled faintly.

"Now, you dratted boy, leave Mr. Sitting Bull alone. He is a rising star among the Lakota; he and another new one, Crazy Horse. They are important men, almost as important as Red Cloud, and a lot more important than you'll ever be."

Wiley himself was limping now, but there was gameness in him. Thus they proceeded another hour into late afternoon, all the while penetrating into wild and haunting beauty. Far ahead, the peaks of great mountains loomed gray in the late sun.

At last they came to a branch. Here a creek rushed in from the east, down an intimate side valley. Wiley led them up the creek through dense cottonwood that formed a natural barrier here, and then out upon a lovely but rugged meadow dotted with aspen groves. He seemed eager now and summoned Lame Horse.

"Now, tell the great Sitting Bull that this is where I kept my stock. I am sure the dratted Crow took most of it, but I have some wanderers that won't stay put here. If the great Lakota would like to sit down and smoke a pipe and trade, why, I'll be most happy to sell horses priced most reasonably —"

"Which way did Crow go?"

"Well, you have to look for tracks now. I had about thirty animals, so look for a large trail. The Crow camp, last I knew, was over on the Stillwater — a long one-sun ride, or maybe two short suns."

The mare, in her home pasture, refused to go farther and happily cropped the lush grasses near the creek. Hannah slid off, pain shooting up her legs as her feet touched the earth.

The three weary prisoners sank gratefully into the cool grass while the Sioux divided, looking for horses among the crags of the surrounding slopes and finding no animals at all. But one found Wiley's artfully concealed dugout snugged against a cleft of a slope behind a copse of aspen and summoned the others. Hannah was amazed. She had stared right at the place, a hundred yards distant, and had not recognized it as a habitation.

Angrily the Sioux gathered around Wiley.

"No horse," said Lame Horse.

Wiley shrugged. "Dratted Crow got them this morning. You'll no doubt find the trail through the saddle in that ridge yonder."

Sitting Bull sent two warriors to investigate, and when they returned, they jabbered rapidly and with much pointing. They had found the route Buffalo Tail had taken. The Sioux debated heatedly, now looking at the saddle in the eastern slopes, now looking at their prisoners, and then back to the notch that would lead them to the Crow camp and a great horse-stealing raid.

128

All the while Wiley seemed to expand again. This was home to him, more than the road ranch, Hannah guessed. He stood and dusted off his frock coat and tugged his vest and seemed to double in size as he puttered with himself. Then Lame Horse approached.

"We will go after them horse now. Sitting Bull, he let you go. This place, she is Crow land. If it is Lakota land, you would die. You come to Lakota land, we kill you, *oui*? The horse, they are more important. With lots of good horse we chase away the bluecoats and the Crow and all the other dogs."

Wiley was fully inflated now. "You tell the great chief Sitting Bull that Dr. Wiley Smart is glad to do favors for the great Lakota and that he hopes Sitting Bull will remember him kindly and come trade horses — a fair deal for all, is my motto — and will smoke the pipe with me. And we shall hunt down the Crow dogs forever and someday make this the land of the Lakota people . . ."

"You thank Wakan Tanka you alive," said Lame Horse. He turned back to Sitting Bull without translating Wiley's valedictory.

Sitting Bull rode up close to his three prisoners and simply stared, a faint smile creasing his face. He was a riveting man, at once as menacing as a coiled rattler and as benign as a priest. His eye fixed on Hannah first, dwelling on her figure.

Lame Horse translated. "Sitting Bull, he say you good to look at and maybe he come back and try you in the robes."

The chief then extracted a small twist of tobacco and handed it to Linc.

"He say you strong boy, make good Lakota. You come if you want, on horse. Lakota kill your family; now Lakota make new family for boy."

Linc cried. Then shook his head. He couldn't speak.

"Say 'Thank you, I'm honored,' you dratted boy."

"I ain't gonna thank for nothing."

Sitting Bull nodded and turned to Wiley.

"He say he don't wan' lame horses. You cheat Crow and whites, but no never Lakota or he kill you quick."

"A fair deal, a fair deal," replied Colonel Smart. "A pleasure to meet you all and bon voyage."

At that the Sioux trotted east up the long slope and disappeared over the saddle.

It was quiet and cooling fast in the twilight. No one spoke for the moment. Hannah was astonished. She was alive. Her feet were ruined, but she'd recover. There was still a chance. A life yet to be lived.

"Now, then," said the horse trader. "There is the small matter of food. I have some provisions stored in the dugout yonder and will share them this one time — strictly as a favor, of course; that is, if those dratted Crow didn't abscond —"

They trudged painfully toward the little cliff-side dwelling. The inside was snug and rather inviting, with a bunk and table and rock-and-mud-mortar fireplace and some crude shelves, which were now empty.

"Drat them. Nothing left. I had intended to do you a favor and let you partake of my goods. I like to do favors now and then for pilgrims, deserving and undeserving."

"I can imagine," said Hannah. "Do you have a gun? Linc could hunt for us if you do."

"As a matter of fact, I do. I have one carefully cached. But have you earnest? I can't just give the boy my only weapon. I'd never see him —"

"If you want to eat, you'd better give it to him," said Hannah tartly. "He's the only one who can walk."

"Drat it, that's impossible. I won't let him have a gun. I'd never see it again."

"Then yuh go on and starve, 'cause I'm going west now," Linc said, walking out of the dugout and heading toward the Boulder River.

Hannah cut in sharply. "I have your silly earnest. Linc — wait a minute."

"I'd hunt myself, but my feet —" Wiley mumbled. "What kind of earnest? Gold?"

"Gold."

"A double eagle?"

"Yes," she said, annoyed.

"If yuh want me tuh hunt, better gimme a gun while there's light. This is when the deer come tuh drink."

Wiley slid outside, hastily pulled brush away from a cliffside pit, and tore a layer of dirt off the top, along with poles and an oilcloth. Then he reached in. In a moment Linc was fondling a Sharps military carbine, some paper cartridges, and a handful of caps. He loaded the weapon, sighted down it twice, and started off.

"Dratted boy will make off with it now," Wiley muttered.

"Will a shot bring back the Sioux?" asked Hannah.

"Their minds are upon Crow horses."

"Do they come often here?"

"Along the Yellowstone, madam, but not here. They raid settlers in the Gallatin Valley almost as if Fort Ellis didn't exist. Dratted cavalry never catches them."

"And your road ranch? Haven't they raided it?"

"My reputation is such, unblemished, that they have always left it alone, knowing a bosom friend."

"Why didn't they kill us?"

"Perhaps they still will. Your fine tresses will make a lovely scalp."

She shuddered.

"Madam, the double eagle, please. How much gold have you?"

"None of your business!"

"Ah, but it is. I'm prepared to make a deal, a fine, fair deal —"

"Like that red mare."

"Regrettable that you mistreated her in that wild run. Yes, a fine deal. As it happens, some of my stock are loners. Especially a pair of fine, big Missouri mules, big black ones, that live a piece away . . ."

"I won't buy a thing from you even if I could pay any price."

"Why, Miz Holt, I just thought I'd let you know I can outfit you good as new. They cost me a pretty penny, and I'll sell them to you for four hundred apiece, and of course I'd sell the pair only. They are used to each other. Bosom companions all their mule lives."

She stared at him and then began to flirt. "I can't pay with gold," she said. "There must be some other way . . . You're sweet to offer them to me. Tomorrow we'll go look at them."

Wiley seemed to inflate again. "I know just where they are, unless that blasted Buffalo Tail —"

"We'll talk about it tomorrow." She cooed, then pecked him on a hairy cheek. "Now I'm going to soak my poor little feet. Must I do it at the creek, or do you have a nice kettle?"

"At the creek. I haven't much left here since those pirates came. Ah, yes. I am at your service. I shall come to the creek and rub your poor feet, put life into them. And maybe we can put tallow on the blisters, eh? I am inclined to do favors for my fellowman."

She limped to the creek, found a rock still sun-warm, and sat on it. He gimped after her, annoying her slightly. She wanted to be alone. She undid her ankle tops and slid the stiff shoes off. The cool air pained the blisters, but the icy water brought relief. The valley was bathed in lavender dusk, turning the aspen to silver and black. Far above them the layered, towering mountains shone amber in the last summer sun, a streak of revelation. It was the first moment of peace she had known in days.

"Ah! What feet! Miz Holt, I have never seen such noble feet, such elegant toes, such sublime ankles, ankles a man could kiss and kiss, feet a man could fondle and think himself in paradise, happy upon the bosom of the earth . . ."

All this was annoying to her, and the euphoria passed. It angered her, the loss of euphoria, a mood worth more than gold. And here was this mountebank rhapsodizing about her blistered, bloody feet.

She smiled sweetly. "I'm so glad you like them, Wiley. You may do me the favor of massaging them, if you are tender-hearted with my blisters."

"Ah! Miz Holt, you transport me to paradise! Truly a noble creature like yourself knows how to love and comfort and satisfy a gentleman of substance and quality."

He grabbed for her feet and began mauling them vigorously. Oddly enough, it felt good to her.

"Now, Miz Holt, I shall be most honored to massage your calves as well, and of course we shall keep your skirts low so that my male eye shall never see the fair, muscled flesh. I suppose I'll do you no small favor, thus relaxing the heated and overburdened flesh, even as I massage the flesh of my fine horses with strong liniment in hand to bring life and relief to my weary animals. Yes, indeed, I shall be most happy to do you this modest favor —"

"Much obliged, Dr. Smart, but I'll be more than content if you massage my toes and insteps and bunions."

"Well, then, I shall, and kiss your fair ankle in honor of —"

A shot echoed through the twilight. And a second one.

134

"Drat. I was hoping that infernal boy would take his time —"

"I'm starved," she said. "Thank you, dear Wiley. I'll let you massage my feet again. Maybe even tonight if it wouldn't inconvenience you . . ."

"Why, Miz Holt, I'd be enchanted to favor you anytime."

She pulled her shoes back on and laced them.

"Well, then, let's help Linc. I'm sure he'd welcome it, tired as he is. Have you salt?"

"Dratted boy," muttered Wiley Smart.

CHAPTER
TWELVE

Neither felt like walking, but they did, wincing every step. They found Linc a quarter of a mile down the creek, dragging a small doe out of the river brush. It was a heavy load for a boy.

"She came to water and I got her. This, here, is a fine rifle yuh got," he said proudly.

It seemed a long way to drag the deer.

"We could hang it here and just take a quarter," she said.

"We've nothing to hang it with," Wiley replied. There was nothing to do but grab the forelegs and pull. They did, taking turns in the cool dark. The stars blossomed. The air was soft. Here, near the junction of the creek and the Boulder River, the aspen and cottonwood were so thick, they formed a barrier that had kept Wiley's livestock close to his dugout. But soon they were sliding the doe across tall grass and had her hanging, gutted, and skinned. Linc expertly cut tenderloin, and they roasted it in the fireplace.

Hannah was famished. Never had meat tasted so juicy and rich, even hastily cooked and saltless. She had an appetite after hiking for miles and riding many more. She had survived this day somehow!

She eyed the furnishings here. There was only Wiley's bedroll, and little by way of utensils. The Crow had taken some, scorned some. At least the little place would be warm. But it would be a hard night on the earthen floor, and she'd end up even filthier than she was now. They ate the cooled meat with their fingers, their hands and arms covered with juices and grit.

Wiley slumped against a log wall. Only Linc seemed to have any energy, and he devoted himself to the routine of roasting and cutting meat.

"I'm going to the creek and wash," she announced. "Have you soap?"

"No, drat it. I was going to make some."

"Never mind," she said. She would find some sand to scour herself with.

It was chilly in the gloom. The September nights were getting cold, near freezing in the mountains. She shivered, having only the dress she wore for comfort. She unbuttoned it. The creek was icy, but she scooped what she hoped was sand from its soft bottom — it felt more like muck — and scrubbed vigorously and splashed her face. Her hair was so grimy, she despaired and found herself yearning for the kettle back at the road ranch, and a little soap and hot water . . .

"Miss — Hannah?"

The voice in the dark startled her.

"I gotta talk to yuh."

She sat up and hastily buttoned her bodice. "Yes, Linc?" she replied irritably.

"This is secret."

She nodded.

"Spotted a pair of big mules up a draw and around a bend when I was hunting. I thought they were deer; it was getting dark. But I crept up the slope, and there was big mules, like home in Missouri."

She stared eagerly at him now. "One for you and one for me?"

"That's what I'm trying to tell yuh. We could get them and get outa here. I mean, he owes yuh one, for the red mare. And I want the other whether he owes me or not."

She thought about that. These were probably what Wiley intended to sell her — at his own price. She had little choice. He already had five of her ten gold pieces for a worthless mare . . . and the rest wouldn't begin to cover what he was going to ask. "Linc," she said intensely, "I want you to do something. Find out if one or both of the mules can be ridden. I can't walk. I can't get back to my buckboard on foot. But if one can be ridden . . ."

"What are yuh thinking?"

"We can both get away. Please try tonight, Linc."

"Sure, first thing, I'll go try. If I get bucked off, it won't work. But it's my only hope, Miss Holt. I gotta get to the gold camps."

"We haven't any bridles," she said.

"There's stuff around. I've looked. I can rig up something."

"No saddles, either," she added.

"Yeah, those mules got a bony ridge that cuts yuh in two."

138

That discouraged her. "Find something. A saddle or a pad. And as soon as you can. Right now, even. Make some excuses to Wiley and then go."

"Yeah, I will. It's my only chance afore more redskins come and kill me next time."

He vanished in the dark, and she saw light flash from the cabin doorway as he entered. She continued to splash cold water on herself, lethargically, getting her dress and petticoat all wet. But her mind was on other things: mules, harness, food, Red Cloud . . . and hope. If her feet were good, she could walk with Linc to the Bozeman settlement and reoutfit. But they weren't.

Painfully she tugged her high shoes on and laced them. They fit better. The cold water had reduced the swelling. Then she hobbled to the dugout and into acrimony.

"I've told this dratted boy he can't stay here tonight. Too crowded. Tiny place."

"It's cold out and I got no bedroll. Yuh want me to freeze?"

"Now, Miz Hannah, don't you think that boy should leave? We have to, ah, negotiate for livestock."

"Maybe Linc would enjoy sleeping under the stars if he could borrow your bedroll. Maybe that way he could get up early and butcher more of the doe without disturbing anyone . . ."

"If yuh gimme a bedroll . . ."

"One blanket. The other is for Miz Holt and myself."

"I need two. It's gonna freeze out."

"One blanket and canvas I have in the cache," Wiley said. Without waiting for a response, he plunged into the dark and returned with a thick roll.

"Now, then, vamoose, boy. Beat it!"

Linc caught Hannah's eye and grinned slightly. Then the plank door creaked shut on its leather hinges.

The fire burned lazily at the hearth. It was a small, warm place.

"Ah, how snug we are. Dratted boy," Wiley exclaimed. "Now, let's talk about your needs. I'm prepared to do favors, of course, to help you be on your way."

"Well, why don't you come over here before the fire and massage my poor feet," she said.

"Now that's capital, capital." He bounded up and spread the blanket before the hearth while she undid her ankle tops and pulled them off.

"Ah, indeed. Sore hoofs. I am, you know, a veterinary doctor, Chalmers College of Horse Medicine, Paducah, magna cum laude, class of '48. I know something about hoofs, and I'll soon have you galloping. Just call me Doctor." He burped, settled beside her, and grabbed a foot.

"Oh! That's exquisite, Wiley! You're such a dear man. Oh! That feels so good! How you love my little toe. I can tell . . ."

"Ah! I shall balm your toes and metabolize your arches. They don't call me Doctor for nothing."

He rubbed her right foot vigorously, and it felt good. He lifted her skirts a little, until bare white ankles caught the glow of the fire.

140

"Now, dear Wiley, you mentioned some livestock you thought I might have if Buffalo Tail didn't find them. Was it mules?"

"Yes, indeed. Fine strong Missouri mules, from good dray horses bred by giant jacks."

"Hush! I don't want the details, I just want, ah, the proposal." She smiled sweetly. He worked her feet furiously and then crept up her ankles as well with fat, warm fingers.

"That's high enough, Wiley. I am every inch a lady."

"Indeed, indeed. I was saying that while the retail price for these prize mules is four hundred apiece, seven-ninety the pair, I might consider the sale — strictly as a favor to you — at wholesale prices. I enjoy doing that sometimes. Many a pilgrim along the trail owes me — but of course, I never collect. It's part of good business, good reputation."

"You may massage my other foot now, dear."

"Yes, indeed. I shall restore it to perfection. Yes. Now, then. Wholesale. I don't do this very often. Only for special, dear, intimate friends. But perhaps if I sacrifice all profit and accept a small loss for a lady in distress . . . five hundred in gold."

"Wiley, dear, that does seem rather steep. I thought mules run about thirty dollars each."

"Why, Hannah — if I may call you Hannah — where did you ever get a notion like that? These are no ordinary mules. These are half again as big, speedy, powerful, high-performance. What's more, they need less food and rest. They're docile, easy to harness. But — God forbid — if the Oglala should descend on you, the slightest touch of the whip will turn them into racing mules and you will thunder away unscathed, with double the horsepower of any Indian pony."

"That's all very nice, Wiley, dear, but I think that's more mulepower than I need . . . You may massage my calves now for medicinal purposes if you keep my skirts down and don't look. My calves are as sore as my feet."

He jumped up. "I have just the thing. Some Dr. Justice Horse Liniment here that will bring you up to heat." He grabbed a blue bottle.

"I think I'd rather not, dear. You just massage my calves in a gentlemanly way for medicinal purposes and I shall be in ecstasy."

He flopped down again before the fire. "As I was saying," he continued, "these are not ordinary mules. They mean safety and life itself in times of trouble. With a crack of the whip they'll accelerate from nothing to seventeen miles in an hour — imagine it! Why, there's scarcely a racehorse that can move —"

"Well, if you say so, dear. It's more than I need, but I'll offer you four hundred in gold plus the return of the red mare, who is worth the other hundred. That's what I paid for her. She'll grow a new hoof, you know."

He pondered it, massaging vigorously. "Well, alas, Hannah, I cannot. You've ruined the red mare as a trade-in. I'll have to shoot her, you know. Perhaps I could offer ten dollars for her as a favor to you."

Hannah frowned. "I guess I'm not in a position to argue. You have the only livestock around. And my life depends on getting some." She sighed. "All right, five

142

hundred in gold and you throw in the harness for the second one."

Wiley looked shocked. She dimpled coyly. He massaged her calves vigorously and aimed higher. "Now don't be hasty," he said. "Let me ponder this. How are your calves? Shall I relax and repeal the ache in your dear knees?"

Hannah tucked her skirts tightly between her legs. "No, dear, I'm a lady, and even if my knees hurt, you may not touch them. Is it a deal? Two mules and one harness for five hundred in gold?"

"Now don't be hasty, drat it. There may be ways I can help save you money. Four hundred in gold and some . . . favors? I like to offer the best arrangement commensurate with profit . . ."

"Shake on it, Wiley." She held out her hand.

"Well, drat it. It doesn't seem . . . you may be able to save . . ."

He shook hands.

"We have a deal," she said cheerily. "Five hundred in gold for two mules and one harness."

"Well, confound it, I'm not sure it's a good one. I can't throw in the harness."

"We have a deal. Let's go to sleep now. I'm dead tired."

"Well, no. The harness will be a hundred more."

She thought about it. "I'll let it go, then. I'll use one mule and harness at a time and tie the other behind."

"Well, confound it, I was just proposing the wholesale price, not agreeing to it when you grabbed my hand and pumped it. I'm afraid I'll lose money. I think I'd better have some small profit on this — the Bible says the laborer is worthy of his hire — and charge seven hundred. Of course, if you lack the means in gold, we might reach some accommodation, in kind, in services rendered . . ."

"We have a deal, Wiley!"

"Well, no, dear, no deal."

She grinned. "I'll give you a big hug to seal it again."

"Ah, madam, let me favor your knees whilst I ponder it. This is a weighty matter, you understand."

She yawned. "I'm tired, dear. The deal's off. I'm going to sleep now. I'd like the blanket. The room's warm and you'll be comfortable in your bunk."

"Now drat, don't be so hasty. Shall I rub your back?"

"I'm going to sleep now." She pulled away from him.

"If the deal's off, you'll never get to Fort Laramie."

She yawned. "I'll walk with Linc to Bozeman and buy what I need. Or take a stage to Fort Benton and get a river packet."

"Well, ah, I might let the mules go for, ah, three hundred if you'll supply some small, ah, services . . ."

"Good night."

"Well, dammit, I'll give away the mules for one hundred fifty dollars — plus, of course, some small token of your love for a lonely man caught in a terrible wilderness."

"Good night, Wiley."

"You can have them for nothing — harness too — if you'll do the small favor . . ."

"Will you shake on it? Bill of sale right now?"

"Yes, I'll do it. Fine bill of sale first thing in the morning."

"Now."

"I have to dig up a pencil."

Some irritation flooded through her. The old mountebank! She stood and wrapped the blanket around her and walked to the door.

"Where are you going?"

"Outside."

"Well, I'll be waiting for you, make you happy."

She left him there, stepped into the night air, and was glad of the blanket. The cool white of the moon caught a small haystack beyond the little corral. She walked over there, wincing as her blisters rubbed.

She was right. Linc had burrowed a place in the hay, soft and protected from night breezes. His dark form was there, wrapped in canvas in the burrow. She knew she'd join him. It would be a lot better than the dirty floor of the dugout . . .

Quietly she slid into the canvas beside him, trying not to awaken him. But he sat bolt upright.

"Huh? What is it?"

"It's me, Hannah."

"Yuh scared me half to death. Redskins. I thought they'd kill me."

"No, this is much nicer than inside. Do you mind?"

"Naw. I got the best of it. Warm in this here hay."

She snuggled down in.

"I got news for yuh."

"Yes?"

"I went tuh have a look at the mules. Hard to catch, but I got them. They look good, got shoes on. One tossed me off. The other let me sit and ride. You kin have the riding one, and I can walk the other. I'll maybe break the other on the trail. I found halters — ropes, too — and I took them out of that cleft and picketed them down in the Boulder River bottom. Miss Holt, we can get outa here at dawn. Take a quarter of that doe and beat it, and he'll never catch us unless he's got another horse somewheres. He's got that Sharps, though, so we got tuh get off early, afore dawn."

She was delighted. "Before dawn, Linc. I'm too tired to stay awake. You're a dear boy."

"Serves the old crook right," Linc muttered.

CHAPTER
THIRTEEN

There was no one there. Wiley awoke with a start at dawn. The hearth was cold. The little cliff-side dugout was steeped in silence. No one outside, either. He found the haystack in a mess and cursed that irresponsible boy. Hastily he forked it into a rain-resistant dome again, wondering all the while what had become of them. They couldn't be far — it was absolutely impossible for Hannah Holt to walk with her feet paining her as they did.

Scheming woman. Well, he'd fix her wagon. Leading him on, then rejecting him. She could disappear for all he cared. Still, it would have been sport . . .

The boy was gone, too, and that was a relief. Infernal, good-for-nothing, hungry-mouth scum, that's all he was. No doubt from Missouri, where all those fanatics devoured each other before, during, and after the great war. Another quarter of the hanging doe had been hacked off — that meant the dratted boy had fled at last. But where was the woman? Taking a bath, maybe? He would look. She wouldn't be far. He splashed water on his face and combed his black beard and hair.

The silence bothered him. If that woman left, it had to be on horseback. He glanced toward the meadow. Yes, the gimpy red mare was there, and something about that bothered him.

The mules! Hastily he dried his jowls and patted talcum there. He was a tidy man. He brushed off the soiled vest and frock coat and pulled on his high-top boots. Then he picked up the shining Sharps, cartridges, and caps and began a tour.

He cut southeast across the valley toward a notch where the mules always stayed except to water. For some reason they liked it there and scorned the company of his herd. He doubted that Buffalo Tail and his thieving Crow had found them or wanted them. The dream burning in the breast of an accomplished Crow warrior was not slow mules but sleek buffalo runners or sturdy war-horses. Ten minutes later he was peering into the notched valley and seeing nothing. But in the dust were moccasin prints amidst the welter of mule prints. They could have been those of the Crow — or the boy.

Probably the boy's. That half-grown trash had probably stolen his mules, his last livestock! For that he should be hanged. If there was anything Wiley Smart couldn't stand, it was horse thieves. And mule thieves. Stealing a man's livelihood was a shooting or hanging offense. He puffed up in rage and eyed the countryside narrowly, swinging the Sharps around. It was an ideal weapon for a long shot, and he could drop that trash in his tracks at four hundred yards using cross sticks as a bench rest. The faint, dusty tracks led not to the creek

148

but west toward the Boulder Valley. So, then, it wasn't Buffalo Tail!

He stormed back to his dugout, feeling betrayed. Here he had helped wayfarers in distress, succored them, sold them a mare, given them shelter in both his homes, blankets, pasturage — and they had turned on him, cheated him like common thugs, walked off with what was his!

Well, he had a few tricks of his own! He had the Sharps and they had no weapon. And he had transportation, too, although it would take some fine doing. He'd catch them soon enough. It would take them time to load the buckboard up there, harness the mules and all, and he'd kill them before they got away.

He eyed the red mare gimping through the meadow and smiled. Not for nothing had he devoted a lifetime to the sciences of equestrian wisdom. Swiftly he haltered her and led her to a smithy area behind the corral. There in a heap was a pile of rusted, discarded horseshoes, as well as nails and certain other little supplies needful to his trade.

He tied her to the snubbing post and lifted the off-hind foot. It was about what he had expected: the soft horn had split and spread outward, shredded on rock. The interior of the hoof was bruised and cut, the frog swollen and damaged where the horse had repeatedly put her weight on it.

Swiftly he nipped away the mashed and torn hoof wall and then rasped the soft horn with a few deft strokes until it was reasonably smooth. It was like cutting a fingernail back to the quick, and now there was no horn at all left to support the interior hoof aboveground.

He hunted for an old shoe among the discards. There was no time to fashion a new one on the anvil, nor did he need a new one. All he needed was something to last twenty or thirty miles: from here to the road ranch and maybe a little beyond. One by one he picked up old shoes and fitted them against the hoof he held in hand. At last he found a good one, except that the toe was badly worn, which made the shoe weak. But it would do.

From his stores he extracted oakum and a piece of tar-impregnated felt. He cut the thick felt until it was the size of the hoof bottom. Then he yanked the old nails from the shoe and found new ones. He packed the soft oakum around the frog of the hoof and slapped the tarred felt over it until the hoof was covered with a soft bandage that might last a few miles. Then he pressed the iron shoe over that and hastily nailed it in place. He clinched the nails over carefully to lock them in the soft horn. They would tear out soon, but he didn't care.

Then he let the hoof down and stood watching. The mare, used to pain, put no weight on it at first. But he untied her and slapped her, and she bolted away, her limp swiftly disappearing. He smiled, satisfied. How often he'd sold horses he'd doctored like that to the pilgrims on the trail. Many had been so dumb, they'd never even picked up the feet of the animal they were buying. Caveat emptor!

He snorted at the thought of it. If God made suckers and fools, then they should be suckered and fooled

150

until they learned something. A few, very few, had returned to protest after their animals had broken down a few miles away. He gave them short shrift. He'd always written "sold as-is after inspection" on the bills of sale, so they were stuck. Like the Holt woman. She had eyes but didn't use them, and if she got burned, it was her fault, not his. He snorted, collected the mare, and bridled her. His saddle was up at the road ranch, drat it, and so were his spares. But there might be a ragged old horse blanket or two . . .

He hadn't taken time for breakfast, but what of it? Prize mule flesh — well, anyway, healthy mule flesh — was being stolen and he had little time. They'd fetch seventy dollars in Bozeman — enough to stake him to a new life if his plans for staying on the Boulder proved impractical. He gathered the Sharps and led the mare to the corral fence. It was hard for a man his age and weight to jump a bareback seventeen-hand dray, but from the corral rail it was easy.

He turned her toward the Boulder Valley, satisfied that the limp had virtually vanished. It was hard on his legs to ride bareback, and the broad back split him in two. But he found she had a jog that was glassy and ate up miles, so he settled her into that and rode north, vengeance in mind.

From a mile away he spotted movement at the road ranch. Hannah was harnessing a mule. She had had to collect the harness from where the Sioux had left it far to the east. And that infernal boy was sitting on the one mule that could be ridden and looked ready to pull out.

151

She was going to head east, he west, and once they split, Wiley would have a time of it.

It was a grand fall day with a friendly sun that lit the distant, gray bluffs of the Yellowstone. He felt good, and something expanded in him. Wiley Smart was on top of the world. He touched his heel to the mare, and she settled into a slow lope. He chambered a paper cartridge and pressed a cap on the nipple. As always, he scanned the ridges for Indians: it was built-in caution.

They spotted him at three hundred yards and looked totally startled. They had obviously not expected him. Now there was a flurry of action, and the boy began trotting north while Hannah buckled the last of the harness and jumped aboard her wagon and lashed the big black mule. The buckboard leapt up the lane toward the trail.

Wiley reined in his mare and aimed the big Sharps .54 at a rear corner of the buckboard and fired. The boom of that big octagon-barreled rifle wrenched the air and the peace. A great splintered hole appeared in the buckboard planking. Wiley loaded again and shot just ahead of the dratted boy's mule, kicking up a geyser of dirt. The mule lurched and bucked violently, pitching off the boy, who fell in a heap, yelling. Hannah reined to a halt, afraid of the next shot. She was too timid to keep on going. Well, some pilgrims weren't cut out to be thieves.

"You confounded robbers!" roared Wiley. "Mule thieves are scum of the earth!"

Hannah stared uncertainly at the leveled Sharps and stepped down from the buckboard.

"Just who's a thief and who isn't is a matter worth discussing," she retorted crisply. "These two mules, worth sixty dollars, don't even repay what you stole from me."

"Nothing wrong with the mare that a shoe didn't cure," Wiley said. "I've a mind to string you both to the nearest cottonwood branch. That's what we do to rustlers."

The boy stood up. "Go ahead and shoot," he muttered. "I don't care."

Hannah stalked boldly to the mare, but Wiley ignored her. He was more concerned about what the dratted boy might do. She stared at the rear hoof.

"You shoed her, but look at it. The nails are half pulled out already. You're the thief, Colonel Wiley Smart!"

There was fire in her eye.

"Caveat emptor! Buyer beware! If you bought a mare with a bad hoof, that is no reflection on my integrity. A fair deal for all, I always say."

Hannah's glare was so scornful and fierce that it momentarily unsettled him.

"Now there's no cause to look at me like that," he grumbled. His attention turned toward the boy. "This was all your doing, I imagine. Private property means nothing to you. You'll grow up a part of the criminal class, the underworld, not fit for the company of decent men." Wiley waggled the black barrel of the Sharps at him for effect.

"It was my doing," snapped Hannah. "And we're talking about fraud. Yours. I'm keeping those mules to repay what you gypped me out of."

Wiley inflated himself to his fullest. "Madam," he began dolefully, "I grieve to think you hold such an opinion of me. It is a hazard of my occupation. A cross I bear. 'Blessed are those who are persecuted, for theirs is the Kingdom of Heaven,' says the Good Book. I forgive you this unreasonable persecution. My shining light is a fair deal —"

"Stop that!" screamed Hannah. "I am taking this mule! And I'm going to get on this buckboard and go! And if you kill me, you can rot in hell!"

"Yeah, and I'm riding west," added Linc.

Hannah jumped into her seat, snapped the reins, and the buckboard lurched forward. "Hiyaaa," she roared, and the mule rotated its ears backward, heard urgency and threat, and broke into a fast trot.

The boom racketed off the bluffs, and the mule slumped in its traces, quivered, and died. Slowly it sprawled across earth.

It was deathly quiet. A smell of burned powder drifted across Wiley's nose. The boy stood transfixed. Wiley inserted another cartridge, capped the nipple, and swung the rifle in the general direction of the boy.

Hannah slumped in her seat, growing smaller until her head was buried in her hands. Her body shivered. He could see it along her back, the trembling. Then she was crying softly, an anguish such as Wiley had scarcely heard in a lifetime. He stared uneasily, and then with mounting rage at her because his valuable mule was dead.

"Confound it, woman, stop that. You try to steal my mule and I'm forced to take measures. And now you

154

bawl like some wretched child. You owe me for it. Five hundred dollars or I'll turn you over to the law, or string you up myself."

Hannah stared at him through tear-wet eyes. Her cheeks were stained with wetness and dust.

"Five hundred dollars and right now. You won't leave here until you pay it. Nothing I hate more than a dratted —"

"Shut up!" screamed Linc.

"Beat it. Start walking," Wiley commanded.

But Linc didn't. Instead he walked purposefully toward Wiley on the mare. Wiley swung the Sharps toward him, but Linc kept on, skinning knife in hand. Just when the boy was about to lunge, Wiley arced the barrel of the Sharps, catching Linc broadside and sending him sprawling. The boy gasped and curled up on the grass, holding his head as if expecting a shot. Wiley stared for a while, satisfied that no threat came from that quarter.

"Madam, get down off that buckboard and cook some meat. I'm hungry."

She didn't move. Her eyes leaked tears.

"Confound it, I've saved your life, but you don't know that. Your sense of geography is appalling."

She stared at him dully.

"You haven't the faintest idea where you're going. Do you think the Union Pacific runs past Fort Laramie? Of course you do. But it runs far to the south, along the Overland Trail. Not the Oregon Trail.

"Do you suppose you're going to be safe on the Bridger cutoff? Ha! The Sioux are raiding west of the

155

Big Horns, raiding Crow and Shoshone, and once you leave the Big Horn River basin, you'll be back in the heart of the Sioux hunting land where Red Cloud and his Oglala roam and kill any white they see.

"Drat it, woman, just last year the Indians burned Fort Casper. That's where you want to go, anyway, not Fort Laramie. There's a road south from there to the Overland. The railhead's around there somewhere. I don't know where. But to reach it you've got to drive that buckboard through the worst Sioux country of all."

Wiley puffed himself up on the mare, praising himself for doing a good deed and saving a life.

"Just remember that Wiley Smart has done you a favor. I should have let you go east and find out for yourself."

The mule lay in a pool of blood, and green-bellied flies gathered and buzzed. The morning sun glinted on the pooled brown blood.

"You're crazier than a loon to come this way alone," he added. "John Bozeman himself died near here a few months ago, and it wasn't Sioux, either. It was Blackfeet."

She sat mutely in the buckboard seat. The boy stood up and led the other mule to the corral, while Wiley watched warily for tricks. Then Wiley put the red mare in the corral too.

Hannah slumped in the seat. The boy began to tug Hannah's harness off the dead mule. It was a hard job. The animal lay heavily on its bellyband and lines. Eventually Wiley joined the boy, prying the mule up

156

while Linc yanked at the harness. He freed it at last and threw it into the buckboard.

"Miss Holt," said Linc gently, "yuh come on into the cabin and lie down. I'll cook us up a haunch of venison, and then we'll think what to do."

He held a hand up to her, and she took it, managing a wan smile, a smile that seemed different from the practiced one she had flashed at Wiley and Linc before.

Linc held her hand and led her into the cabin, and she tagged along like an unresisting child.

Wiley slowly shoved the wagon back from the mule. They'd have to drag the dratted carcass away soon, or it would become unbearable here. He trudged down to the river and washed, and on the way back he noticed a thin line of white smoke rising from the chimney. The smell of roasting meat was in the air.

Inside, Linc worked quietly. Hannah lay mute and haunted on the bunk, her eyes elsewhere, in another world. She did not resemble the woman Wiley had first encountered. Wiley sank to the bench and waited for food. It was quiet. The morning was warm, and the door was ajar in the sun.

That quiet was shattered suddenly by a sharp *thunk* on the door, a sound Wiley instantly recognized. Linc jumped. Hannah remained oblivious. Wiley knew what he'd see even as he lifted his eye to the sunlit door. A Crow arrow protruded there.

He arose, Sharps in hand, and opened it wider. There was Buffalo Tail on a pony, this time painted for war with great streaks of red and black across his cheeks and powerful upper arms. And behind him, also painted for war and on bright ponies, were fifty or so more Crow warriors — friend or foe, he didn't know.

CHAPTER
FOURTEEN

They sat on their spotted ponies in frightening array, the warpaint like a smear of blood across the horizon. Some wore one or two eagle feathers jutting upward from inky hair. Some wore headbands. Most had buffalo-hide war shields thick enough to turn an arrow. Most had firearms, and those with the shining Henry or Winchester repeaters were holding them ostentatiously. Others had bows and arrows, feather-decked lances, war clubs of rock and bone. A few had battle-axes or hatchets they could throw with deadly effect. On the shields were sacred symbols painted in carmine and white and black, totems, personal medicine. They were stripped down to their breechclouts and their copper skin, greased with warpaint, glinting in the bold sun. The ponies beneath them, some painted with black or white handprints and war symbols, trembled and snorted and pawed, aware of some raw, male force in their riders and matching the mood with their own high-strung nervousness.

Wiley stood in the door. Hannah joined him, quaking. Linc turned rigid.

"Aieaaa . . . it is Dr. Smart," said Buffalo Tail.

Wiley expanded some, tugged his frock coat. "Ah! And how is my esteemed and noble friend and boon companion, Chief Buffalo Tail?" he replied with a slight tremor in his voice.

"I am no more chief than you are doctor," responded the headman. "But I *am* a war leader."

"Why, sir, I am a doctor of veterinary medicine as expounded by the late Professor Justice of Paducah."

"A medicine man. A doer of temporary miracles," mocked Buffalo Tail. "You have slain a mule and brought a lame mare back to soundness."

Hannah detected the acid in the headman's tone, and it surprised her. She hadn't thought much about Indians other than to suppose that they were barbaric. It surprised her that they could laugh or weep or mock or tease or joke the way white people did.

"We are looking for a small party of Sioux. They came through here," said Buffalo Tail. "And when they left, they had two shod horses."

The colonel inflated again. "Infernal thieving redskins," he roared. "Yes, they came through here and stole my remaining geldings, and may they rot in Hades for it — or the redskin version of it, anyway."

There was a malicious look in Buffalo Tail's eye.

"Their headman is Sitting Bull. They were Hunkpapa. He's supposed to be a chief of all the Sioux, but who believes it? I roundly chastised the brute and told him to be off."

Buffalo Tail turned solemn. "Sitting Bull. He is a great Sioux war leader, a worthy enemy of the Absaroka

160

people. You should not speak of him with contempt. He is worth a dozen Professor Smarts."

Wiley deflated slowly.

"Why does a slain mule lie here soaking the ground with blood?"

Hannah spoke first. "Because he shot it. He was afraid I would take it instead of the red mare."

"Theft, pure and simple. The dratted woman was stealing it and that other one in the corral. Horse thieves, scum of the earth, except yourself, my friend."

Buffalo Tail leered at him. "And why would she steal a mule? It is a poor thing compared to that red mare, yes?"

"Why, the dratted woman ruined the mare running from the Sioux."

Buffalo Tail slid off his painted war-horse and walked to the mare and inspected the rear hoof. With a hard yank he pulled the loose shoe off, tearing horn. The felt pad and oakum dropped out. He stood up and barked a command.

"Harness the other mule to the woman's wagon. You are all coming with us to our village. It is not safe for our white friends to be here alone. We hear of the death of white men everywhere now that the bluecoats are gone."

"If yuh think I'm going, you're wrong," grumbled Linc.

"Killer of my son, you especially will come."

"Yuh gonna scalp me for killing him? But maybe I won't die so easy."

Buffalo Tail nodded. Two of his warriors slid to the ground and advanced to the door. It frightened the boy.

"I'll come temporary," he muttered, and walked out.

Hannah slowly overcame her dread of these wild men with all the weapons of death at hand. They had evoked a fine terror in her lungs and stomach, but now she was slightly more at ease. Miraculously Wiley's other mule was being led to her buckboard, and the reluctant horse trader was grumpily slipping collar and hames on it. She dreaded the Crow camp and whatever awaited her there. Would she be used by some greasy, painted brave? She quailed at the thought. And yet . . . a wild hope pierced her as well. She would be free of Wiley Smart. She might even — was it possible? — get this Crow leader to take her wherever it was where she could get aboard the Union Pacific.

Buffalo Tail seemed to stare right through her. Was her beauty attracting him? she wondered. She started to smile — the hard smile she had practiced to perfection for so long — but she didn't. Instead she felt some sense of reserve, a fear of artifice that might lower her in the esteem of this red man whose gaze pierced her.

"Thank you for caring about our safety," she said quietly.

He didn't acknowledge it.

The wagon was hitched. She climbed to the seat, looking for a last time at this lonely road ranch, at the cleft of the Yellowstone Valley to the north, at the majestic peaks to the south, and felt a sudden, odd sadness.

"You ride. The boy and Colonel Smart walk," said the headman. "Or the horse trader can ride the red mare."

Wiley sputtered some, and hunted for his saddle. But the Sioux had taken it.

"Walk fast," said Buffalo Tail. "Long way to go. Two suns with this wagon."

Wiley turned to Hannah. "Their village is on the Stillwater — maybe thirty miles, maybe more."

They traveled east along the Bozeman Road, which angled southerly away from the Yellowstone River and cut through the majestic foothills of the Absaroka Mountains. It was slow going, and the two score warriors paced themselves to the mule-drawn buckboard and the walking of Linc and Wiley. The mule struggled up long slopes and down long slopes, the buckboard pressing against the breeching.

This was a war party, and without instruction, vedettes spread out to the front and flanks, alert for the rampant Sioux, who had gone on an orgy of raiding ever since the soldiers had left. These Crow did not ride in a disciplined column as the soldiers did but in free-forming clots of silent warriors.

Their fierce garb, weapons, and lean, coppery bodies still frightened Hannah. She noted that the Crow seemed leaner and redder than the Sioux. But there was comfort in it, too, for these were the enemies of the Sioux and possibly her protectors, though she wasn't very sure of that.

Here in the heart of the Crow domain, the land was breathtaking. High, blue mountains jutted into the southern heaven. The plains undulated like washboard, with live creeks lined with cottonwood and brush along every bottom. Game was everywhere, but the party didn't stop to take any. These warriors would make meat later, she concluded. It was that easy to find. The Crow seemed to exist in a kind of savage paradise; certainly a place that fulfilled their every need.

The party did not even slow down, and Hannah could see that the Colonel was very weary, even though he plodded on gamely. She drew beside him.

"You may ride for a while," she said coldly. "I'll walk."

He boarded the creaking buckboard gratefully, and she paced beside Linc, glad to stretch her legs, even if her feet began to sting instantly. She didn't care about the Colonel and owed him nothing; it had been an instinctive gesture. A few hours earlier she had itched to shoot him as dead as a man can get with her hideout revolver, which now bumped softly against her thigh.

"When you're tired, you can drive, too, Linc," she said.

He didn't seem grateful. "They're making me go east, and I want tuh git west," he grumbled.

Buffalo Tail reined in beside them. "Why do you let him ride? Does he deserve it?"

"No," she said.

"I do not understand the ways of whites," he said. "Why didn't the Sioux kill you?"

"I don't know. Some wanted to. They were looking for horses and Crow to steal from."

"I don't know why they didn't kill you," the headman said. "They tried to steal horses from our village and didn't get any because we were ready and very brave. They ran east, but the trail was cold this morning. I came here to see if you were alive. It is strange."

Hannah glanced back at the slow-moving buckboard, now out of earshot. "It was Wiley," she said. "He told Sitting Bull he was a friend of the Sioux and an enemy of the Crow and that he could show them your trail from his other place."

Buffalo Tail began to chortle. "And now you let him ride the wagon."

"Maybe he saved our lives doing that!" she replied angrily.

Buffalo Tail rode silently a moment. "No pride. White men have no pride. It is better to die bravely. No Absaroka would try to save his life that way. Offend the gods. Die in shame or live in shame."

"What's wrong with living?"

He laughed softly. "You chose the wrong road to live."

That cryptic remark chilled her.

Her feet, unhealed from the long march two days earlier, began to flame badly, but she kept on walking. When Wiley relinquished the buckboard seat to Linc, Hannah climbed up beside the boy because every step now was beyond what she could endure.

"Linc," she whispered, "come to my tent tonight. We'll sneak away and get to Bozeman somehow. I have some plans."

He nodded.

They stopped at a creek in mid-afternoon, and Buffalo Tail gave them a bit of jerky and chokecherry pemmican. She found she liked both, although the greasy pemmican had a vaguely stale taste. The bits of nourishment did not even begin to satisfy the hole in her belly.

Linc remained quiet and sulky while Wiley — stymied by language barriers among the other warriors — tried to engage Buffalo Tail.

"The dratted Sioux pretty near had our scalps," he told the headman. "Infernal savages, led by that brigand Sitting Bull, a common horse thief."

Buffalo Tail smiled politely.

By the end of the day they were only halfway to the Stillwater village. Buffalo Tail halted on a nameless creek close to where the Bozeman Road forded it.

The wooded flat was idyllic, protected from wind, offering firewood and shelter and thick grasses for the horses.

Her supplies had been pillaged, but the tent remained, and she had one blanket. She set about pitching the tent and making a nest for herself. A muffled shot racketed through the twilight, and moments later two mounted warriors dragged a heavy five-point elk into camp.

She ate elk tenderloin that night with a greed that amazed her.

The camp seemed to organize itself. Two warriors closely guarded the ponies, which now included the mule. Others scrubbed off war paint with river sand, or rolled out their robes. She was not threatened or molested in any way and soon overcame her dread of walking among them. She made herself useful by gathering firewood and helping with the cooking. But she dreaded the moments she was out of sight of Linc or the headman.

There was no one to talk to. She tried Linc, but he snarled at her. Wiley was a bore, and she avoided him. He seemed hollow and small unless he was trading or suckering someone. A man without a self, she thought. Buffalo Tail seemed almost unapproachable. His two closest friends, Thunder-in-the-belly and Many-women-laughing, always seemed to be beside him, saying few words, like a captain with veteran sergeants, she thought, except that Buffalo Tail never gave orders. The headman seemed to gain his authority from other things, a prowess of some sort.

In her tent in the blackness of a moonless night she took stock. She was still close to terror, and she caught herself wondering when a war tomahawk would crack her skull in two, or when an arrow would sink into her chest and she would know for a fleeting moment that she was dead. But they had not touched her. Oh, why had she ever started on this mad journey?

Deep in the night there was a soft scratching on the tent flap. She was alert instantly.

"Linc?"

She pulled the flap aside, and a small dark form crept in.

"Yuh really want to go? To Bozeman?" he whispered.

"Yes!"

"Can yuh walk? All the way to Bozeman?"

The question daunted her. "I'll do it," she said grimly. "I thought we could walk in the creek now, so we don't leave footprints. It goes down to the Yellowstone, doesn't it?"

"Yuh know how hard that is — over them slimy rocks?"

"Yes. I'm ready if you are. I saved some elk, enough for two meals."

"Yuh think I should try for two horses?"

"There's double guards, Linc . . . the Sioux . . ."

He thought about that. "That's a point," he muttered. "How we gonna dodge 'em when they come lookin'? The creek's the first thing they'll follow."

She was impatient. "What time is it?"

"Reckon after midnight by the Big Dipper."

"Then we can be miles away by dawn. I can walk, Linc. The cold water will help."

She crawled out. It was serene, and the great, black dome of heaven was strewn with chips of ice. There was no moon. She tied the laces of her ankle-top shoes together and slung them over her neck.

"I guess I'll stay here," he whispered. "Buffalo Tail'd kill me if he catches us."

She was annoyed, but her mind was made up. "All right, then, Linc, you stay. But I'm going. Just don't tell anyone. That's all I ask."

"How yuh going to live? Eat?"

"I'll figure that out when I get back to Wiley's road ranch."

She did something impulsive then, and later wondered what had impelled her. She hugged him.

He squirmed and then stood quietly while she clung to him. Then she let go, slipped silently toward the burbling creek, and lowered her feet gingerly into the cold, rippling water.

It was immeasurably slower going than she had imagined. She had hobbled scarcely a hundred yards when a foot skidded on a slippery round stone and she hit the water with a resounding splash. The shock of cold hit her, drenching her skirts, pouring through her camisole. She bolted up, water sluicing out of her hair, and began to giggle. She couldn't help it. She was bone-cold, soaked, and feeling hilarious.

"You take noisy baths," said Buffalo Tail quietly.

Her heart tripped. She stared up at the silent headman on the creek bank.

"Oh!"

"When you finish, go back to your tent. It is not safe here. You are lucky you do not have an arrow in you."

She laughed, stood, and began wringing water from her clothes while he waited. Then they walked back to her tent, and he left her there. She found spare clothing in her trunk and hung the rest outside on the tent to dry.

She awoke refreshed. The mountains were rosy in the long light of dawn. She had scarcely noticed the good earth before, but this morning she felt it around her and smelled its fragrance and noticed the late-summer asters. And it struck her that she didn't know why she was in such a rush to get to Saratoga Springs. Had she actually believed it was the only place in the universe she might be happy?

It was quiet. A lark sang. The sun warmed to gold and caught the eastern flanks of the mountains and gilded them. She watched, knowing that this ordeal was transforming her, though she didn't know how and wasn't sure she approved.

When she returned from her toilet at the creek, she found them cooking pieces of elk skewered on green willow sticks over their tiny, efficient fires. Roasted meat was cooling for her, and she gnawed on it lustfully. The warriors glanced at her occasionally. They had been faceless at first, but now she began to see individuals. They talked in their own tongue and ate elk until they were sated.

She watched Wiley eat his. He seemed unkempt now, the frock coat stained and shabby. His tidiness had vanished, and he reminded her of some snake-oil peddler hawking tonics in dusty villages, vibrant before a crowd, a hollow shell when alone.

They were off quietly, and she turned back to look. The place tugged at her. But the big black mule was fresh and feisty and full of the devil, so she devoted her attention to the driving. Linc and Wiley walked cheerlessly, and the warriors, paintless now, filed along the deep-rutted road, occasionally passing debris left by westbound pilgrims, and small grave sites marked by weathered planks with a few scorched hieroglyphics on them. She wanted to stop and read them, but the column never slowed.

Today, as yesterday, there were vedettes out protecting the group from surprise by the deadly Sioux. The country changed little. The trail was never level but negotiated steep slopes constantly. From the tops of ridges she could see the Yellowstone Valley far to the north at ever-widening distances.

By mid-afternoon the party reached the ford of the Stillwater, which was a wide, shallow stream, narrowed now by late-summer drought. Here they left the Bozeman Trail at last, turning south into a lush, increasingly rugged country. The clear stream raced through heavy brush and groves of cottonwood. The pace quickened, for this was home.

Ahead, smoke hung lightly in the transparent air, and when they rounded a wide bend, some seventy cowhide lodges met her eyes, golden cones with smoke-blackened tops, arrayed in orderly circles. Off on the other side of the river a great herd of ponies grazed, guarded by boys. The news of their coming had preceded them, and now they rode through gawking children, doeskin-clad squaws, and younger women in bright trade cloth, then on toward a larger lodge. These people were silent, for the party did not return wearing the paint of victory. They pressed on to the great lodge at the south end of the village. Its door flap faced east, the sacred direction of the dawn sun.

"Where are we going?" Hannah asked Buffalo Tail.

"To the lodge of the chief, who will welcome you."

"I thought you were the chief."

"I am a little chief, a war chief. But this village is that of Two Coups."

"Is he chief of all the Crow?"

"No. There are many villages. There is another village half a sun away."

An aged, wrinkled man with a feathered baton stood at the great lodge. Two Coups awaited them.

CHAPTER
FIFTEEN

The thing that impressed Hannah instantly about Two Coups was his dignity. He stood gravely awaiting the village guests before his great, painted lodge. His iron-gray hair, shot with white, hung loose and at shoulder length. A fringed elk-skin shirt hung over his protruding belly, and fringed elk-skin leggings covered his bowed legs. Around him was a mass of noisy spectators, barking mutts, racing naked children, but he was an island of quiet.

Hannah drew up the reins and halted the buckboard. Linc scowled, a hatred and fear of all Indians alive in him. Wiley seemed to expand again from a soft, round ball of flesh into a southern cavalier, vibrant and strong.

Buffalo Tail talked with the chief in Crow, and Hannah understood none of it except that at one point the chief's brown eyes stared long and hard at Linc, and an angry murmur went through the spectators, who stared and pointed at the boy, the killer of Horned Moon. Then the chief's eyes rested on her lingeringly, and her buckboard, and finally on Colonel Smart, who stood transformed. Wiley was someone they knew; she could see that, and as they discussed the colonel, faint grins emerged on shining faces.

Hannah stared around her. It was her first experience of an Indian village, and she was too fascinated to be afraid. She knew, too, that the Crow had been friends and allies — more or less — ever since the fur-trade days. There were odors — of cooking stews, drying meat, leather and hide. And when the breeze quartered from the east, the rank stink of urine and feces caught her. There was the acrid smell of sweat, too, and sweet sagebrush and horses. Everywhere was riotous color, young women in amber, carmine, and cobalt trade cloth and ribbons.

Then Buffalo Tail was welcoming her in English. "Chief Two Coups welcomes you to his village and hopes you will enjoy your visit."

"I am grateful to be here, protected from the Sioux and among friends," she said. Two Coups seemed to understand, though Buffalo Tail translated. She remembered that these people harbored whites among them for decades and could probably understand English. The chief nodded kindly.

Then Buffalo Tail addressed Linc. "Chief Two Coups welcomes you to his village but with a heavy heart. You will stay in my lodge. My woman will stay with her sister. She will not stay with the killer of her son." He paused. "I have told the chief that your tongue is true, that you are brave, and that your mind is like the mind of the Absaroka. He said I can do with you whatever I wish. You will stay in my lodge."

Linc reddened angrily. "I didn't ask tuh come here. Yuh forced me. All I want is tuh get out of this redskin land."

174

Hannah glared at the ungracious boy.

"Your words are true," said Buffalo Tail dryly.

Then Wiley broke in, beaming.

"My dear friend, the great Chief Two Coups," he began, "how glad, how enchanted I am to enjoy the hospitality of the noble Absarokas . . ."

Hannah, annoyed by the windbag, glared at Wiley, who by some magic had inflated himself. The grimy frock coat now hung smooth and clean; the dirty brocade vest now fitted perfectly; scuffed boots turned shiny; baggy pants hung straight; slumped spine was now ramrod erect, and dull hair glistened. Even his voice turned young and mesmerizing. How such a thing could happen, she didn't know. The Indians would call it medicine, and a kind of medicine it was.

"I am Colonel Wiley Smart at your humble service," he continued as Buffalo Tail translated as best he could. "I come to share the secrets and mysteries of the equestrian arts, to teach the ways of the horse, to install health and speed and bravery into the sturdy ponies of the Crow people . . ."

The crowd picked some of this up as Buffalo Tail translated.

"I am, indeed, Professor of Equine Science, Doctor of Veterinary Medicine, having imbibed the wisdom taught at the Doctor Justice School of Equestrian Disciplines, Frankfort, Kentucky. And indeed, a colonel in the militia, having as my specialty the scientific adaptation of horse to military strategy and tactic — in short, a master of horse cavalry and horse logistics . . ."

The last overloaded Buffalo Tail's abilities, but he conveyed the drift.

Colonel Smart paced back and forth, and around him a small arena formed. The Crow were fascinated, and so was Hannah.

"And being in possession of these priceless secrets and refined arts, which date back to the Pharaohnic secrets of the Egyptians, I intend to convey them to the bosom of this noble and friendly people, the greatest of all tribes. Before your very eyes shall I select your fastest ponies and teach them to run still faster . . . heal the sick, mend the wounded, transform the spindly and poor into great war-horses and buffalo runners . . . teach your young people equitation and dressage. But most of all shall I instill speed in your mounts until they can outrun any horse of any other tribe."

He plucked from some inner recess of his frock coat a turnip watch and waved it back and forth on its chain. "With this, this magic medicine of white men, I can count time and speed." He swung it gently on its pendulum chain, like a practitioner of Mesmer's hypnosis.

"When I am done, your ponies shall run faster than any Sioux pony!"

"Aaah!" exclaimed the Indians. This was something to hear!

"Think upon it, my fine red friends," he intoned. "After I have imparted my rare secrets from the ancient world, my medicine, your beasts will race like the wind and strike like lightning. Crow war parties will overtake

176

the slow Sioux, and you will win great battles and engagements, steal to your heart's content . . ."

He paused, tugged at his frock coat.

"Nor is that the end of it, my fine-feathered friends. After I have performed my labors your buffalo ponies will be fleeter and braver than ever and run down the fastest cows. Your outlaw horses shall be gentle and tractable, suitable for even an old squaw; your young ponies shall learn faster, for I shall impart ancient secrets of horse discipline unheard of in the councils of the red man, secrets scarcely known even by cavalry bluecoats.

"And even that is not the end of it, my dear friends. For under my veterinary care these ponies shall blossom and grow strong; I will heal the weak and cure the unsound and instruct them in manners."

Buffalo Tail stumbled along with all of this, and most of the Crow were getting enough of it to follow along.

"And as an added benefit there will be days of racing. We shall match the fleetest against the fleetest. And before I am done, we'll all know which of your ponies runs fastest and farthest, and this village shall become famous among the Absaroka people."

Wiley had lit fires of ecstasy, especially among the warriors, for whom fleet and enduring horses meant life or death.

"Now, of course," he added, eyeing the Crow shrewdly, "I will do all this for free, absolutely gratis, for nothing, save a few paltry meals and a corner of a lodge someplace. It will be an act of friendship and help secure my own fortunes against the marauding Sioux.

But if, eh, you should feel some pleasure, some small gratitude, some exiguous token of your esteem would be warmly welcomed, eh, a spare pony or two . . .

"And, of course, during the match races we shall make wagers, eh? Those who discern fine horseflesh most keenly shall become the richer, eh? And even the losers shall have a dandy time, after all."

He beamed beatifically. Chief Two Coups nodded skeptically, said something or other, and dismissed them. His eyes followed Wiley.

Buffalo Tail leered. "My friend Wiley Smart intends to clean out the village," he said.

"My gracious, you harbor evil thoughts," Wiley replied. "No, I am a poor wandering knight come to bestow horse sense upon the Crow for better or worse, and have no more private appetites than a monk."

Buffalo Tail turned solemn. "You will stay in my lodge, Slippery Tongue. I trust the madam here will cook for you and the boy. I will be elsewhere, with my wife."

That news did not appeal to Hannah, who had gradually been forming her own plans. But she said nothing for the moment. She had never been inside an Indian lodge and was curious. Maybe she'd delay a day or two; maybe she'd even cook for Wiley and Linc and whoever else lived there.

Her plan was simplicity itself. In the morning, or maybe the following morning, she'd be on her way east. Here she was free of Wiley's grip. She would take the mule, and there was nothing he could do about it. She'd drive up to the Bozeman Road and start east

178

again. But first she would learn more about where she was going. Wiley had disconcerted her, saying the Bridger cutoff was no more safe than the Bozeman Trail, and Fort Laramie was nowhere near the Union Pacific. Well, she'd see about that.

She had something else in mind too. She meant to hire a Crow escort. If Buffalo Tail rebuffed her again, she'd try others. Still, she wasn't sure of all this. Was she a prisoner here or a guest?

The welcoming ceremony was breaking up. Buffalo Tail nodded, and she wheeled the buckboard around and followed him to his lodge. Brown children peered at her shyly or darted in front of the mule, and some older children tagged along behind, whispering and giggling and pointing at her. Few Crow had much experience with white women, she supposed.

The lodge was some distance from that of Two Coups. She watched uneasily as a youth undid the harness and led the mule away toward the great pony herd. Would she ever see it again? How could she even tell one of them she wanted it brought to her?

She needed to relieve herself but there was no place to do so, and for a moment her dread of all savage Indians lanced her. But then she trudged east from whence the smell occasionally came and found semiprivacy in the bushes. There were squaws nearby but no men. She continued on down to the river and scrubbed, feeling grimy. There was no privacy. The village seemed to have none except inside the lodges, and maybe not there, either. It was all a blur of dogs, brown horses, women on their knees scraping hides, naked boys darting, older ones playing war games with miniature bows and arrows. And happiness. This was a sunny place, a place of joy, some sublime mating of the Absaroka and the land that nourished them.

She returned uneasily to the village and would have been unable to say for sure which lodge was Buffalo Tail's but for her wagon parked there. It was untouched. She began to understand: the Crow were great thieves but not from any guest in the village. That was no doubt unthinkable.

She found Buffalo Tail, relaxing, sharing a pipe with several others, Thunder-in-the-belly among them.

"May . . . I talk with you?" she asked hesitantly.

He stood solemnly. He was a man impervious to her, she knew. She had used wiles successfully all her life, on white men. But this Indian was different.

"I thought I would leave tomorrow. If I am permitted."

"Go if you wish. Nothing stops you."

"Would I have the mule?"

"Is it yours?"

"Wiley Smart has not agreed to it."

He smiled. "It is better than the red mare. I will tell Wiley Smart you have traded him the mule for the red mare."

"Thank you."

"There is nothing to stop you except death."

"Death?"

"You and the mule will die. Sioux war parties ride along the road made by Jim Bridger, where you are going. They have attacked us there, and the Shoshone too, and when you take that road south out onto the prairies again, the Sioux are as thick as summer buffalo. They torture expertly. Their women like to torture white women to see if white women are strong. But maybe you would enjoy that, being strong to them before you die."

She colored angrily. His faint mocking pierced her.

"Mr . . . Buffalo Tail. Would you take me to the iron horse? The railroad? As I have said, I would pay you."

"Pay me what?"

"Gold."

"What would I do with gold?"

"Why, buy things. Guns."

"If Absaroka lose their lives escorting you, will gold buy them back?"

She didn't say anything. Something in his tone mocked her. Something in her sagged, and she didn't want to badger him further.

"I will go alone, then," she said dully. Saratoga Springs seemed farther away than ever.

"Stay here awhile. Several suns, anyway. And we will talk about it."

"But no decision now?"

"It is a thing to be talked about and discussed by the elders of the council. Many Absaroka might die taking you" — he smiled — "to the Iron Horse, as you put it."

"I will wait, then."

"The Absaroka way is to think about things. And visit the medicine man. If the medicine is good, I might take you. Tomorrow I will take you to Three Hawk Feathers, and he will look into your heart and spirit and the future."

"My spirit?"

"Yes. He will talk to you. I will translate. Maybe you should not go. Maybe this place in the east where you want to go is bad. Maybe you are on a bad road to a bad place. He will tell you."

"I'm stuck here, then."

"You are not stuck. You are a guest. You may go when you wish. We do not tell guests what to do. If the guest does not like the Absaroka people, the guest can go away."

She reddened. Somehow she had gotten off on the wrong foot with him. "I will do what you think is best," she said contritely.

There was no one in the lodge. The fire at the central pit was out, but it was not dark. The late-afternoon sun shone translucently through the scraped cowhide skins that had been sewn into the lodge cover. She was surprised to find an inner lining attached to the lodge poles. It extended above her head and was anchored by rocks at its base. It was comfortable here, oddly quiet and private, even in the boisterous camp. There were buffalo robes, soft and heavy; a backrest chair one could lounge on. She realized this was a lodge in mourning; she didn't know how it differed from other lodges, but there was no color here now, and it seemed austere. Perhaps Buffalo Tail's squaw had simply taken such things to her sister's lodge, although there were parfleches filled with her host's possessions.

She fetched a clean yellow dress from the trunk in her buckboard and changed into it, fearful that someone would invade her privacy or see the lump in her damp petticoat where her revolver was. But no one did. She felt better. She might cook now, but where was food? Where was meat? She had a few things, some beans and airtights of vegetables, in the buckboard, but she'd need those for her trip.

She lifted the door flap aside and blinked in the long sun.

"Ah, Miz Holt, a word with you, if I may. Privately, away from all these dratted savages."

Wiley had receded into himself again, looking unkempt, ungroomed, unclean. He leaned against the buckboard, idly fingering the harness that had been tossed onto it, and she wished he'd keep his grubby hands off her things.

"What have you to say that can't be said right here?" she replied.

"Why, nothing. I thought I might treasure your beautiful company."

"What do you want?" she asked sharply.

"Why, just to tell you that opportunity is upon us. The gates of heaven have opened to us, and providence shines. We shall be rich; we shall enjoy an outpouring of life-giving wealth. Yes, right here, and in a very few days. All it will take is a bit of that gold, and a most fortuitous partnership. Do you have it?"

"That's not your business, Colonel."

"But it is! It is! With it we shall turn a hundredfold profit, reap the rewards of the just! Renew life in tooth and spirit!"

"This has something to do with the horses."

"Yes! How discerning and intelligent you are! Indeed. These Crow redskins are horse-mad. Horse-delirious. They'd rather steal a nag than eat! And race horses until they die. And wager, yes. They are famous sporting people, wagering all they have on a race — robes and rifles and horses and squaws and daughters and medicine totems and lances and saddles . . . They are mad gamblers, and that's where, ah, a little refreshing opportunity comes."

She was beginning to understand.

"You want a stake for the wagering."

"Ah, you are bright today, Miz Holt. Yes, indeed. But not I. We. For you shall share and share alike. Never has fortune glimmered so near, so bright. The pilgrims on the Bozeman Road — they gave me a modest profit but nothing so grand as this."

She sighed. "And how are you going to do this?"

"I am a born horseman, of course. I shall cull out the slow, train the fast, groom the best. And with my watch here — see the second hand there? — keep time. A secret just for the two of us, eh? The infernal Crow won't know the running times. Eh? That's for us to know. And, of course, I have small, effective measures to slow competing quadripeds down."

"Cheating. No, Wiley."

"Now don't be hasty! Think upon it. Mounds of wealth. And best of all, when we scram, we'll take the fleetest horses, those few that have come under my training and timing, and they'll never catch us. We'll be miles away and gaining all the while."

184

"We are guests here," she said sharply.

He paused cheerily. "Well, I'm offering you the chance of a lifetime. El Dorado. A little gold put up for a sure thing —"

"No!"

"Well, I'll proceed without you, then. It'll take a bit longer, a little more confounded work. Too bad. I had meant to offer you a full partnership. Think about it, madam."

CHAPTER
SIXTEEN

The next morning, Wiley crossed the Stillwater on stepping-stones the Crow had placed in the stream, and wandered south to the village pony herd in a lush meadow rimmed with cottonwood. Crow youths tended the herd and worked with individual horses. A warrior, armed with a rifle, stood guard on a hill. With Sioux all around, the village was watchful.

Wiley had formed the rudiments of a plan. He was going to get out of there and make a fortune at the same time. The road ranch was dead. His livestock gone, some of it right here in this herd. The Bozeman Road was likely to stay closed. But whites weren't the only chumps. He'd skin what he could from these redskin chumps and then vamoose.

He'd find the fastest horses and train them. Run a few match races and acquire some Indian wealth — buffalo robes, a rifle or two, things he could trade. Then he'd take the fastest horses — three, perhaps, one to ride, one spare, and one for packing — and leave the whole village behind in a cloud of dust. And just for safety he'd disable the others.

The more he pondered it, the more he refined and weighed the contingencies. What if there weren't any fast horses in this village? Fast enough to outrun the Sioux, for instance? Well, then, he wouldn't go through Sioux country. But if he did find some fast mounts, he'd head south to the railroad and the Colorado mining camps where his fortunes would shine once again. Or west to Virginia City or Last Chance Gulch, but he really didn't like this latter prospect. The Montana digs would be full of pilgrims who had traded with him and come up short. No, Colorado was better.

A Crow youth waved, and Wiley beamed cheerily as he walked through the herd like a cavalry colonel on an inspection tour. He felt positively dapper and dusted off his black frock coat. The herd wasn't very reassuring. The mustang ponies were fall-sleek and starting to hair up for winter, but not built for speed. Most had high withers, narrow chests, and low, small rumps. It was a rare pony that had good, straight legs. Most were cow-hocked. But their hoofs were excellent, small and hard. Mustangs didn't need shoes. Mother Nature had ruthlessly weeded out the ones with soft hoof horn over the centuries, and the weak had perished.

These were multicolored, too, and Wiley didn't like that. Solid color was a sign of breeding, he believed. But these were paints and dapples and spotted horses with shaggy manes and tails that nearly touched the ground. He'd remember to roach the manes and clip the tails of his racing mounts. There were mares and yearlings and colts here, and a few stallions.

The horses milled as he strutted through them. Like many good horsemen, he could wander through a herd without upsetting it very much. Something in him conveyed calm to the wary animals.

Drat it, there was scarcely a speed horse in the bunch. These were rubbish, worthless beasts good only for feeding dogs or pulling travois and not much else. But, of course, these were not the buffalo runners . . .

Off to the north, where the Stillwater Valley broadened, was a separate small herd, better guarded. And here were several of the village warriors grooming their animals. These were the prized buffalo runners and war-horses that the Crow treasured above all else. Some warriors put such stock in these ponies that they tied the animal next to their lodges at night to prevent theft. These were the fastest, bravest, strongest horses, able to keep pace with a racing buffalo — it always amazed him to realize that a buffalo could often outrun a horse over any longer distance.

Jauntily he strolled among them using his sharp trader's eyes to assess each animal. These were broad of chest, powerful through the stifle and forearm, and he judged that some showed promise as speed horses. A trained buffalo runner was worth, in Indian terms, a great deal, because it brought its owner riches in the form of meat and robes to trade, as well as prestige in the village.

He spotted Buffalo Tail ahead and, with him, the old chief himself, standing beside a tall gray horse. It was the horse that caught Wiley's eye rather than the headmen around it. It was no Indian pony at all, but something one might see at a racetrack.

Apparently the Crow were waiting for him, so he joined them.

"A majestic animal, a fair flower of the equine race," he proclaimed.

Buffalo Tail explained. "Chief Two Coups thought you'd like to see him, Slippery Tongue. This is the fastest horse in the village, maybe the fastest in all the Absaroka villages."

"Built to run," Wiley agreed lasciviously.

"He was a gift to Two Coups from a trader," Buffalo Tail continued. "The trader wanted us to bring robes. He also wanted Two Coups's youngest daughter." The headman smiled. "Two Coups accepted the horse but did not give him the daughter, Frozen Water."

"The chief is to be congratulated," Wiley said. "This animal has blood."

"I do not know the word *blood*. The trader used words I do not know. He told Two Coups this horse was half thoroughbred, half Virginia quarter-mile racer. Strange words to Absaroka, but speedy horse."

That explained it, Wiley thought, a getaway horse, a horse to speed him straight through the Sioux nation, a horse to leave Two Coups or Red Cloud eating dust. He beamed.

The chief muttered something. "He says do you want to see it run?" Buffalo Tail explained.

"Indeed, indeed," exclaimed Wiley. "And bring me the next best in the village."

The village had a running track of sorts, a stretch of level, soft riverbank ground without any badger or gopher holes in it. Wiley paced it off. Three hundred yards, he judged. The warriors with the fastest buffalo runners appeared with them, and Wiley studied the competition. There'd be no races today. Just a little running. They were handsome mounts, these buffalo runners, but he didn't doubt that Two Coups's stallion would take them all. He frowned. The chief's horse being so superior, there'd be not a soul in the village willing to bet against it. That might make the betting a little sticky — unless he did his wagering on the preliminary runoff races.

A boy was up on Two Coups's gray, guiding it with a hackamore. As he warmed the horse a great crowd gathered. This was something the Crow loved, and the whole village collected in the meadow.

Then the gray was ready. They had their own way of beginning, from a standing start, but Wiley wasn't interested in beginnings. He positioned himself midway on the track where he could study the animal full-stride. The chief dropped his hand, and the gray bolted forward, running easily in an uncollected gallop. Wiley saw what he needed to see. The animal was fleet but wasting energy. He would devise a few things . . .

One by one the buffalo runners were raced past him; slower, but good distance horses with bottom. Most of them didn't run in any collected way, either. He doubted that any could win a race against the powerful gray. Still . . . there were ways and means. One stallion, a solid chestnut, looked promising. It was a big one, sixteen hands, and it dwarfed the mustang ponies. It might make a great packhorse when the time came. It belonged, it turned out, to Many-women-laughing.

190

His third mount he'd select later. He wanted a fine spare, a rotation horse along, but he didn't know which.

"Buffalo Tail, my bosom companion, would you convey my thinking to your esteemed people?"

"Maybe I'll say your thoughts rather than your words, Slippery Tongue."

Dratted Redskin, Wiley thought. Buffalo Tail's eyes glinted.

"My fine-feathered friends," Wiley began in stentorian voice, strutting back and forth before them, "in a week — ah, seven suns — I shall declare a day of races and feasting, a day of wagers, and we shall see the fastest horses run. I promise surprises, upsets, amazing victories, the unexpected. Bring your plunder to wager — your robes and rifles and squaws and daughters . . ."

Buffalo Tail leered.

"And don't count on an easy victory by Two Coups's gray. For I am a professor and doctor of horse science, and I will heal the sick, make the slow fast, make the lame sound, and, ah, postpone the day of judgment. 'By their fruits ye shall know them,' the white man's book says, and so you shall know me."

He wasn't sure Buffalo Tail was conveying the pitch, but it didn't matter. Both Hannah and Linc stared at him, mouths agape. He smiled slyly.

"Yes, I am colonel as well, chief of the graycoat militia in the late war, and I will teach these ponies to go to war. They shall bite the Sioux with their teeth and kick the Blackfeet with their hoofs and lord over the ponies you steal."

He let Buffalo Tail catch up.

"Yes, medicine. I have horse magic and the threefold blessing of the Confederate Army, and the sun, and the Doctor Justice School of Horse Science of Lexington, ah, Frankfort, to lay at your feet . . ."

He preached a considerable sermon in this vein and then dismissed them. Two Coups stared long and hard, then walked back to the lodges.

"Chief Two Coups's medicine is bad about you," said Buffalo Tail. "Two Coups will watch you closely."

Wiley nodded graciously. "When Two Coups sees what I do with his splendid horse, he'll remember me for life," Wiley retorted. "I need riders — strong boys, mostly — who understand English."

"None do. But I'll stay and tell them."

"Thank you, my fine friend." He turned, hunting for Linc, but didn't see the confounded boy. Linc was going to be recruited for some jockeying. He understood English, and that was half the battle.

"Now then, Buffalo Tail, I am in need of some long strips of tanned leather as wide as my thumb, and some thong. I mean to make martingales for these animals. They run with their heads flying every which way, and we'll remedy that. You do that and I'll go fetch that dratted boy. He was here a moment ago."

Buffalo Tail nodded and went off to cut some leather while Wiley strutted back to the lodges. What golden opportunity! What an army of innocents abroad on the Stillwater! What ripe plums, juicy fruits! Apples in Eden!

He frowned. He needed tools. A rasp and nippers particularly. That gray racer was long of toe and showed it. Just by shaping the hoof he'd add speed. Well, he'd seen a few Green River knives, and there was also that lazy orphan's skinning knife, but getting hoofs trimmed would be no picnic.

He found Linc at the lodge with Hannah. The boy was still preternaturally silent and sullen.

"My fine young friend, the chance of fame and fortune and spiritual and moral command of life is upon you. You shall be my assistant manager and trainer and jockey, all for such grand rewards — horse, rifle, saddle, pemmican, robes — as good Providence shall provide."

"Yuh talk too much."

"Hear me out, young whippersnapper. Would you like a fleet horse to take you west? One with royal blood coursing its veins? You shall have it if your heart is pure and your bosom unsullied."

Both Hannah and Linc stared at Wiley in disgust.

"Come along now, and help me rig some martingales, and then you'll put those ponies through their paces."

Linc sighed but followed Wiley across the stepping-stones and into the meadows. Wiley headed for the big chestnut. If he was going to make a race, he'd have to bring that chestnut up to some speed close to the gray.

The chestnut's hoofs needed work, and Wiley set about it vigorously, laying aside his frock coat and vest. A knife was all he had but it was honed, and he chiseled horn with it.

As the day progressed, Wiley turned into a whirlwind. He soon had Linc plus some Crow boys fastening crude martingales to the buffalo runners and riding them in figure eights, while he whittled at hoof and horn and bitted several horses with Hannah's bridle. He was a man obsessed, and the sheer energy of his work began to draw spectators, including Hannah, who watched it with a disturbed look on her face. But Wiley was too busy to notice. The Crow youths were eager horsemen and good. Most had gentle hands, which surprised Wiley. He had expected the Crow ponies to be hardmouthed. Two Coups appeared several times, bemused by the intense activity.

Linc worked sourly but soon forgot his miseries and was absorbed by the disciplining of the horses. The boy rode bareback like the Crow boys and was comfortable enough. Buffalo Tail was on hand much of the time to translate and keep an eye on Linc. The headman studied the white boy frequently, as if trying to decide something in his mind. But whatever it was, he kept his counsel.

By the time the shadows were long, Wiley could see some progress. He had the hoofs of all the fastest horses — six in all — roughly trimmed. The gray racehorse had stopped tossing its head and had started to run in a collected lope and to change leads properly doing figure eights. The chestnut was even more collected but slower. Also, it was showing bottom, as tireless at the end of the day as it was at the start. Of the others, a seal-brown bronc seemed a good prospect if he could be gentled down and muscled up.

194

Wiley was as tireless as the horses, galvanized by the hopes that now consumed him. At dusk, when he approached Hannah's buffalo-stew pot, he was as vibrant, youthful, and shining-eyed as a boy.

Buffalo Tail spent little time with his white guests, preferring to be with his squaw and her sister's family. Which suited Wiley just fine, for he had not given up his intention to use Hannah's gold for betting, and he needed privacy to work on her.

"Tomorrow we start ponying. The next day we start loping. And I'll begin some time trials. I shall need your help to record times — we'll use a bit of charcoal for want of a pencil — and the day after that, some trial heats.

"And after that we'll clean 'em out. If not with the gray racer, then in the earlier match races between the buffalo runners. Confound it, woman, haven't you sense enough to get in on a sure thing?"

"And what if I lose?" she said.

"You won't lose. I have ways and means."

"To fix the races? Is that what you're saying?"

"What gave you that infernal notion? It runs against the ethics and disciplines of my profession. If I did that, I'd risk my reputation, drat it. And then where'd I be? You and that orphan would tell the whole world that Wiley Smart is a, ah, malefactor. No thank you. I offer a fair deal to all comers . . ."

"No, Wiley."

"Confound it, you can triple your investment. And we'll have mounts to flee here without being touched."

"Yuh mean steal horses," Linc said. "That's what you're figuring. Yuh got Two Coups's racer in mind for that. Yuh try that and the whole Crow nation will be after yuh and kill me and Hannah too."

Wiley glared. "Small thinkers lead small lives," he said. "With a mind like yours, you'll spend the rest of your earthly tenure shoveling out stables. Think grand, think mountains!"

"Yuh think robbery is what yuh think."

"Stay here, then. Don't come along. I am offering you the chance of a lifetime, golden and foolproof."

The boy had a way of twisting everything around, making him look felonious to Miz Holt. Well, he'd get that gold, even if he had to turn her upside down and shake it out of her . . . The thought amused him.

"What would I do with my buckboard?" she asked.

"Abandon it. Miserable thing, anyway. You'll have riches galore, why worry about it? We'll take the nine fastest mounts — three apiece — and they'll never catch up. What's the buckboard? A trifle. Let me wager it and the harness against a rifle or good robes or saddles — things we can trade at Fort Laramie. If you won't sport your gold, then put up the wagon and gear. There's squaws itching for your dresses — put them up. I'll tell you which horses in which races . . . Divide your plunder, pack the little you need, and wager the rest . . ."

Hannah seemed disturbed. She paced the small confines of the lodge, around and around the cook fire.

"Do you really think we could outrun them?"

"My good woman, you haven't seen the like. And with spare mounts to rotate, we'd be the whirlwind."

"What could go wrong? What do you see as the dangers?"

"I'll tell yuh. The danger is that Two Coups'll come after yuh breathing fire 'cause yuh stole his prize pony."

"Drat it, boy, you stay out of this and let your elders decide. You're too young to calculate risks."

"And who says a fast horse is all yuh need? Maybe bottom is better; horse keeps a-going. Maybe maps and knowing the places to water and spots to hide in, the land, and all — that's better than a fast plug."

Wiley smiled scornfully. "My dear young man, do you suppose I haven't thought of all that and taken measures, prepared for it?"

There was a long silence.

"I don't know," Hannah said. "But I don't have to make up my mind yet."

CHAPTER
SEVENTEEN

Linc enjoyed working the horses. Each hazy morning he reported shortly after dawn to the meadow along the Stillwater, and each morning Colonel Smart was already there, hard at work with the buffalo runners.

"If only I had a snaffle bit," Wiley mourned. "My kingdom for a snaffle."

But there was none, and Wiley made do with the hackamores the Crow used to control their ponies. Linc had swiftly become expert with them, controlling the mounts as easily as he did with metal bits. Wiley had stopped scolding him and seemed to take a child's delight in the progress of every animal. He had taken to gently addressing Linc, the Crow boys, and even the horses.

The owners of the buffalo runners were usually on hand watching quietly, as was Chief Two Coups. Wiley concentrated most intensively on the gray racing stallion. Each day Linc took the gray through some slower gaits with the martingale in place, and then, when the colonel felt the horse was moving head-down and collected, he removed the tie-down, as he called the martingale, and let the gray run flat out. The results were plain to see. The horse was smoothing out, running in a flowing streak with no waste of energy. Wiley began to time the runs with his big turnip watch and looked increasingly smug. So did Two Coups, who monitored the progress carefully.

Linc was oddly happy. Somehow he had become the principal jockey. Wiley used the Crow boys, too, but he could not instruct them and used Linc on the gray and the chestnut.

The chestnut was actually Linc's favorite horse. He sensed power in the animal as he rode it, a driving force that could carry a rider for miles. As the days passed, he almost forgot his goal of getting to Virginia City. And forgot, too, that he had been forcibly brought here. The task at hand was so challenging that he was soon infused with Wiley's excitement, and he began to see Wiley as a kind old rascal.

The other horses progressed even faster than the gray. They had been an undisciplined lot, eager and fast and brave but half crazy, too, and less controlled by the hackamores. Some ran with head painfully high rather than seriously with head low and stretching forward over the ground. Wiley had his watch out frequently now, clucking happily, recording times with a piece of charcoal.

One thing puzzled Linc. The colonel was accustoming each horse to a metal bit and bridle, a white-man rig taken from Hannah's harness, even though these Crow didn't use bridles. Wiley put Linc to work teaching neck reining as well, even though the Crow didn't steer their horses that way.

Increasingly Buffalo Tail sat in the grass watching the training. His eye was frequently on Linc, until the boy grew flustered. Finally Linc could stand it no more.

"What yuh staring at?" he demanded.

"Come walk with me. The colonel will let you go for a little while."

Reluctantly Linc slid out of the saddle and walked beside the headman. It had something to do with shooting Horned Moon, he was sure. Maybe Buffalo Tail was going to kill him now. He didn't much care. It didn't matter what happened to him, with his ma and pa dead. They walked on down to the river until they had left the village behind. It was quiet in the hazy fall sun.

"You are a lot like my son Horned Moon. You have as many winters as my son."

Linc waited, puzzled.

"Do you like it here?"

"Yuh got a nice village. Don't know about winter in those skin lodges of yours, though."

"They are warmer than you think. And they have inside-skins tied to the lodge poles too."

"That what you come to talk about?"

Buffalo Tail shook his head. "No. Not that. I lost a son. My only son. And I want a new one."

Linc's heart tripped. Not that. Not that.

"You have a good heart and a straight tongue — unlike one white man I know."

Linc frowned. "Yuh mean to keep me here?"

"I don't know. You are young to be on your own in the mining places. It would be good if you were to stay here a year and grow up more."

"Yuh mean I can't go even if I want."

"I didn't say that. I said it would be good for you to stay."

Linc pondered. "But I don't want tuh stay in some Injun —"

"I will ask something of you: Stay here for a while and make up your mind later."

"What for? I got tuh get going."

"My son is dead."

That subdued Linc. "Look — I — it just happened. That's war, taking horses."

"I know that. Your father and mother are dead. That is war too."

Linc sensed where this was heading and wanted no part of it.

"If yuh think — if you're fixing to make me a son, adopt me —"

Buffalo Tail's gaze rested on the boy. "It is considered a great honor among the Absaroka," he said dryly. "Even more an honor that I would adopt the killer of Horned Moon."

"But —"

"It means that we Absaroka honor you more than you imagine. But you don't want to spend your life here with the Absaroka. You want to go to your kind. Very well. You could do that. You will be free to come and go. No son is a prisoner. If I adopt you — there is a sacred ceremony and a name-giving — you will always have a home and a father and" — he paused — "a mother."

"Yuh mean someplace to come? Home, like?"

"Once you are a son and have taken the Absaroka name the medicine men shall give you, you will always have a home. All the village will be your brothers and sisters and mothers and fathers and uncles and aunts. It is the greatest honor we possess, making you one of us."

"Yuh mean I could stay some and go somewhere and come back?"

"That is what I mean. But I would like you to winter here for now. And in the spring, if you wish, go to the gold camps. But if you go, you will not lose your Absaroka father. You will come back to the village of Two Coups and be a son and brother."

"But what if them others don't want a white-man boy —"

"It is a private matter. If I adopt you, the village honors that. If you have to defend yourself from Absaroka boys, the village honors that, too, and hopes you will fight them. But they fear you. You have killed an Absaroka."

Linc felt strange stirrings of the heart. "I don't know. Would yuh let me think on it?"

"Yes. But I will take you to a medicine man. We have several. And he will test your heart and tell you the medicine. Will you do that much now?"

Linc decided he would. He'd talk to the old smoke and feather hoodoo man and see what he had to say. The old man would probably think up some big-medicine name, like Elk Feathers, and hang it on him. Well, that would be all right too. Getting a new ma and pa, even if redskin ones, wasn't half bad, especially if he got hungry.

"I like it here. This is a right nice place," he allowed.

Buffalo Tail's eyes lit up. "I will take you to meet others. You will have many friends. I have told them that your tongue is true. Tonight, after Wiley Smart is done, I will take you among my people."

"Mr. Buffalo Tail, thank yuh."

They walked back to the meadow. Wiley was fuming.

"You lazy boy, there's ponies to train and you go off lollygagging —"

"I took him to talk of man things."

"We've got races coming. My fine friend, Buffalo Tail, put your sporting money on those two runners there, the big chestnut and the long brown. Those two are shaping up champions. That's a private tip, my friend, a token of my esteem, a little favor just between us."

"I get the feeling, Slippery Tongue, that you run match races the way you trade horses."

Buffalo Tail wheeled away toward the village before Wiley could fashion his riposte.

"Blast it, what did he corral you for? Trying to fix a race?"

"Naw, adopt me."

"Confound it, stop pulling my leg, boy. Get your lazy behind up on that stallion."

Linc did, but he wasn't concentrating on the task at hand. Furtively he peered at the village across the stream, the cones of lodges set in orderly circles, life flowing through them.

He wondered what his Indian name might be. Would he have a choice? Could he be a warrior, a fighting one, and steal horses from Blackfeet? Count coup on some enemy?

". . . confound it, boy, you're not paying attention. Now collect that dratted horse. Get him to change leads by leaning toward it . . . Stop your mooning."

He wondered how he'd look in a war bonnet. How he'd get the precious eagle feathers. Would his new mother help him? He'd never seen her, at least that he knew of. Would she hate him? How would he get along with her?

He did not dine at Hannah's stew pot that evening. After the training, Buffalo Tail came for him, and soon Linc was meeting Buffalo Tail's wife, Before-dawn-light. She was a tall, graying woman, solemn now, and Linc wanted to be anywhere else. But she served him good steaming buffalo-hump roast and then served him something else — a small, brief smile as if to say she'd meet this new son halfway.

By the time darkness settled upon the village and the lodge fires glowed through the skins, Linc had met more bronze people with strange names than he could remember. Among them were several shy and dazzling girls who seemed as much at a loss for words as he was.

He scurried into Buffalo Tail's lodge and burrowed into his robes. Hannah was an inert form in hers, and Wiley snored softly, muttering incoherently, in his. The intimate arrangements had been faintly embarrassing at first but no longer were. It seemed all a part of living in a Crow village.

Linc lay in the thick, dark buffalo robes wondering. Someone wanted him, even if it was Injuns. It puzzled him. Why would they want him — the killer of Horned Moon? Tears came. It was a bleak thing to be twelve and have killed someone. He snuffled in his robes and hoped that Hannah didn't hear him.

Maybe if he took a Crow name and got adopted, he'd feel like someone else. Maybe he wouldn't have to think about Horned Moon anymore. Maybe those old spook medicine men would bring back Horned Moon's ghost to haunt him. Maybe he oughtn't let them do all that stuff to him. They were fooling with demons and hobgoblins and devil stuff that could wreck his life . . .

He lay frightened in the dark, not knowing what to do. Buffalo Tail, and even Before-dawn-light, seemed to hold out their hands to him. But he didn't want that; he wanted to go where his ma and pa were going, do what they started to do before the Sioux — The memory of his mother's last scream burst upon him and he shuddered, and then sobbed quietly, finally drifting into a haunted sleep.

Hannah was not asleep, either. Wiley's proposition haunted her. He seemed so sure! They'd be free and so well mounted that the whole village would never catch up! On her way east at last! And even having outrun the Sioux!

But that was only part of it. Linc was right too. What of the rest? Would they know the land, the hiding places, the water? Was she a good enough rider? What good were fast horses if she slowed them all down, flapping along, barely hanging on? What good were fast horses if they were caught camping or sleeping in the night?

But there was something else troubling her, too, something she scarcely would have cared about only a few days ago. The buffalo runners that Wiley proposed to steal were the wealth and the lifeblood of the village. She had asked Buffalo Tail about them, and he told her they were prized by all the Indian people of the plains. A good buffalo runner was essential if a hunter hoped to bring meat to his family, and hides and bone for tools. A village without buffalo runners was a village on the brink of starvation.

And here was Wiley, planning to steal the nine best horses in the village, including the racing horse of the chief — the chief! — as well as the buffalo runners. What might that start? A war! The Two Coups band would mount itself as best it could and come after them relentlessly, recklessly, counting on sheer persistence to make up lost time. And here they were, guests in this village, treated kindly as friends and allies and fellow victims of the Sioux . . .

Hannah sighed restlessly and then was amazed. Here she was, caring about the fate of wild Indians, feeling ashamed of Wiley, who was snoring ten feet from her.

She wondered how he'd steal them all, those closely guarded treasures of Indian life. And then she knew. Even now Wiley was insisting that the horses be kept on the meadows at night where they could graze. Usually

206

they were tied at night to the owner's lodge. Of course, there were special guards out there now. Wiley would have to trick or overpower them somehow.

She listened to Linc and wondered what the matter was. The boy sniffled and whimpered in the dark. Eventually it stopped, and the boy drifted off to sleep.

The lodge was pleasant at night. She spotted some stars through the smoke hole. There was a kind of half-light that let her make out the outline of things. The air was gentle, with the smell of earth and robes and ashes and smoke in it.

What was she thinking of? Did she want to spend the rest of her life in a dirty Indian camp? Sleep on the hard earth with nothing to soften it but a robe, as she did now? Live with that latrine smell whenever the breeze brought it? Wear clammy skins instead of satins? Banter with savages instead of civilized people?

She was suddenly angry with herself, wondering how she had succumbed to the savage enticements of this place. She stirred uneasily. She was growing weak! She was abandoning everything she had learned about getting ahead in the world!

What was all that compared to taking a few horses from some savages? Didn't they all think that horse stealing was a game, anyway? She'd gone soft! She'd gone dotty on that Buffalo Tail, whose strong, lean, coppery body with its rippling muscle disturbed her every time she looked at him.

Tomorrow she'd no longer be a spectator. She was going to ride. She was going to make very sure she could sit a horse and run with the wind. She'd slit an old skirt and sew it into culottes so she could ride astride. She'd begin to weed out the wagon and bundle the load she'd take with her. And when the day came — or night, rather — she'd be ready!

She fell into an easy sleep at last, having made her fateful decision.

CHAPTER
EIGHTEEN

With the passage of two more days Wiley knew for certain which of the village ponies were the fastest. He had timed them separately, run them in heats, and then repeated it all until he was sure. The village had eleven fully trained buffalo runners and a few green ones. He intended to take nine, three each for Hannah, the boy, and himself.

Of the other two, one was fast but notably balky and narrow of chest besides, which meant he probably wouldn't last long. The other was simply slower, a disciplined animal that no doubt was fearless alongside the cruel horns of the buffalo but a laggard nonetheless. He would leave these. He had thought to loose-herd them ahead but gave up the idea. It might slow them up or provide the Crow with fresh horses in a chase.

Nine buffalo runners! That was a young fortune in its own right. The runners were as prized by whites as by Indians and could be traded for mountains of goods. With nine runners a man could rebuild a lost fortune, begin anew in the horse-trading business. There might, of course, be a small problem — that infernal woman and the boy might suppose they owned their three horses instead of borrowing them. But what were a weak woman and a gangly boy? He would deal with them, especially after he had traded for a revolver of some sort. But even if he lacked a weapon, his big fists would do nicely. He'd try for a rifle, too, just to keep any vagrant Sioux at bay.

Nine buffalo runners! Why, he didn't even need to run match races or wager on them. Why bother? Why load up those fleet animals with all that loot, buffalo robes and all, that would only slow them down? No. This mobile, four-footed wealth was perfect for his purposes. And as long as that dratted woman wouldn't part with her gold, it was hardly worth the bother to run a lot of rigged races just to skin some Crow out of some hides.

Yesterday she had shown up in a split skirt and had taken to riding. That was good. Most of the Crow youths were riding naked, which had startled her, but soon she had that fake smile pasted all over her delicious mouth and was riding beside them.

But she was making progress. If she was going to come along and not drag them down, she would have to become accustomed to fast horses. This was a run for the money! He watched her approvingly. She noticed and waved cheerily. It stirred him. Maybe on this little jaunt — if that dratted orphan wasn't along — he could have her . . .

He wasn't at all sure Linc was coming, anyway. He seemed to cotton to Buffalo Tail and even the squaw. The trouble was, he needed the stupid boy. The brat was a good horse handler and could skin a deer faster than Wiley could skin a pilgrim. Without that boy he might have to take fewer buffalo runners — and that would be dangerous.

Hannah rode up on the long brown. "How'm I doing?" she asked.

"Miz Holt, capital, capital. A fairy princess on her steed."

"Are we going to get away soon?"

"Shh," he cautioned. By now half the village watched the training. There were Crow everywhere, and most of them were young warriors picking up Wiley's tricks. Any one of them might understand English.

She wasn't chastened. "Tell me how I'm doing — for a long run."

"Woman, you flop too much. Collect your body and collect your tongue. The more you flop, the more you wear the horse down."

"You may know horses, Colonel, but you don't know women." She smiled fetchingly and rode off.

Dratted female. He'd have her soon . . . He watched a Crow boy and Linc line up their horses at the start of the track, and when they were ready, he dropped his arm and they were off. The orphan was good, down low on his mount, little burden on it. He held back the spotted pony a bit, letting the Crow boy get the edge, but then toward the finish the Crow's pony flagged and Linc's surged ahead. The boy had some racing sense.

Linc rode the sweat-soaked stallion back and reported to Wiley. "This is Buffalo Tail's own runner," he said proudly. "He wants me to ride it and work with it."

"You and that headman are pretty thick."

"He's going to adopt me," Linc said proudly. "It's big doings, and I'll become a member of the whole village."

"When's that coming?"

"He hasn't set the day yet. But it's a big feast day. First they take me to a sweat lodge and soak out all the old spirits and burn sweetgrass and sage and stuff, and those old medicine men sing a bunch of prayers to their heathen gods.

"And then the old boys give me a Crow name. I don't even know what it is yet. And then we come outa there.

"Buffalo Tail, he says I got tuh come out naked and with all them women standing around, and I says no, I ain't, I gotta have a blanket, and he just smiled.

"After that's a big dance and whoop-de-do with all the drums banging, and then a big feast for the whole village."

Wiley beamed. "Ah, so you'll be the star attraction. The whole village, you say? Ah, indeed . . ."

"Yeah, just about everyone. It's big doings, real important to them, making me a son and a brother. And then Chief Two Coups, he speaks a long stem-winder welcoming me, and then I got tuh think of something tuh say back, and it goes on like that all night . . ."

That bit of information delighted Wiley. At last he saw the way to bust loose easily. He'd leave the kid here — as a decoy. He didn't need the dratted kid, anyway, with the Holt woman learning so fast.

"Ah, my fine young friend —"

"When yuh sweet-talk like that, you're always after something, so I'm telling yuh no right now."

"Don't be hasty, drat it. I'm about to set the great racing day. And I'd like you to tell Buffalo Tail to set your adoption the day before . . . The races will follow the next day and be a part of the big celebration, eh?"

"Yuh got a good idea. I'll tell my pa."

The boy wheeled on Buffalo Tail's spotted runner and splashed across the river.

Now it was coming together! The big adoption shindig would be the perfect cover. There might be a horse guard or two watching the buffalo runners — maybe not even that — to get rid of. Probably they'd have rifles Wiley could snatch. He'd have Hannah Holt all alone, and nine fast nags. They'd do it when all those savages were dancing and prancing. Ah, it'd all come together! His luck had returned! On the night of the adoption dancing and feasts, he and Hannah would put forty easy miles betwixt this camp and themselves, and widen the gap every day!

On the next occasion when Hannah paused to rest herself and her mount, Wiley stepped over to her, making sure they were out of earshot.

"It's about set," he whispered, "and as near foolproof as mortal man can devise."

She fetched him her best dimple and waited.

"The adoption will be a big celebration in the camp. All eyes will be on that addlepated boy, who thinks he's going to be the next Red Cloud. And when the light is low, my dear, I shall escort you to the herd of runners, make short work of the night guard — who won't expect danger from me — and we'll be forty miles away before they discover it . . ." He chortled raucously.

She seemed disturbed. "But, Wiley — what if these people . . . what if they turn on the boy and kill him? They'll be mad, you know."

"Since when has an infernal, lazy boy kept you from your destiny?"

"Well, I'd feel bad if Linc —"

"Pah. Hush. Trust in your benefactor. I will deliver you on a flying carpet to Fort Laramie, and you can proceed from there to the railroad with a dozen cavalry troopers at each shoulder and kiss them all before you board your varnished Pullman east and settle down into wine-colored cushions in your private compartment . . . And when you do, you'll remember Colonel Wiley Smart forever, and the favor he did."

She laughed, a tinkling waterfall of amusement.

"I think I'm doing you the favor," she retorted.

"Ah. Eh, indeed."

She eyed him so provocatively that he wondered if it was an invitation.

"Ah. One more matter. Go light, my dear. Only one blanket. Abandon your rags. Flying carpets can't carry more baggage than yourself."

"But, Wiley — everything?"

"Almost."

"But my dresses! Shall I get upon a Pullman in rags? In this? Show me how to make a small pack for my spare horse. Please, dear Wiley."

It was too much to resist. "Later. Not now. When we have a private moment. There's a way to make a roll of

214

your tent and crack it over the withers and make it stay. A surcingle and a diamond hitch. And you can put your little nothings into it."

"I have lots of little nothings," she said. "Thank you, dear. You're sweet."

She rode off, and soon he was putting another buffalo runner through the prescribed disciplines. Wiley wasn't sure his routines would add much to the speed, especially with no grain handy to feed the ponies up to prime. But they would be collected and economical and endure hard use longer. And, of course, they would be better muscled. That would be the edge that would whisk them safely away and past the very noses of the Sioux.

Idly he watched Linc splash his spotted horse across the river and canter up to him. The boy seemed excited.

"Buffalo Tail says the day after tomorrah. I tole him I wanted to get adopted, be a Crow like him and his squaw, and he says he's got a happy spirit and he will, and he'll get his squaw busy on the feast. He's got tuh make meat first and get the medicine men lined up and powwow with Two Coups and all. I tole him yuh wanted to run the races the next day to sort of celebrate, and that was fine with him. He liked that. So we're all set, and the races will top it off."

Wiley beamed, and his black beard jutted forward. "You'll make a splendid thieving Crow yet, boy. That was a piece of work."

It was done, then. Odds and ends to take care of: the delicate matter of a weapon; teaching that infernal woman how to pack a horse without a packsaddle; a look at some hooves. Maybe discombobulate some of the faster horses they'd leave behind . . . a little injury, a pebble jammed against the frog. A little locoweed if he could find some. He'd think of things.

That afternoon Two Coups, flanked by two medicine men with scowling faces, summoned him from the meadow. They stood at the village side of the river. Wiley hurried across the stepping-stones to meet this strange delegation. They looked solemn, and that vaguely alerted him to . . . what?

The chief motioned for Wiley to follow. The man radiated power and a will that was not to be brooked. Wiley dusted his frock coat and trousers and proceeded, wondering whether to corral Buffalo Tail as translator.

"We will smoke a pipe," said one of the elders in English. Wiley was pleased. He would be able to talk to the old chief, who plodded ahead on his bowlegs.

Two Coups entered his lodge first and walked ceremonially around the fire pit to take the place of honor. The old, stooped men followed and sat cross-legged, flanking the chief. Wiley wasn't sure of protocol, but he followed around the fire pit and sat at further remove, eyeing the decor of the lodge — scalps, two hanging rifles, a medicine bundle draped from a lodge pole behind the chief, robes, bright trade blankets, and various dyed parfleches.

The Crow said nothing. From a soft-tanned pouch Two Coups extracted a long medicine pipe with a bowl of reddish pipestone and a long hardwood stem that

216

was wrapped in sinew like a Crow bow. Leisurely the old chief tamped a twist of tobacco taken from another pouch into the bowl and lit it with an ember. Then he saluted the cardinal directions, earth and sky, and handed it to the medicine man on his left. It was a long ceremony, and Wiley was impatient, eager to return to his nags. But there was no speeding up a redskin, he thought.

Not until the whole bowl was burned and the chief had knocked the ashes out was anything said. Then the chief began to rumble things and pause while the old medicine man translated.

"The chief welcomes you and asks the blessing of sky and earth spirits upon you . . . The chief wishes to inquire about the races. And about the training of these horses."

Wiley didn't like the tone of all this. The little smoke wasn't exactly friendly. He straightened up — the dratted sitting was putting his legs to sleep — and nodded slightly.

"Tell Two Coups I am honored to be at his village, and I thank the mighty chief and mighty warrior for his welcome." Wiley wondered if he was laying it on too thick.

"The chief asks of your purpose here."

"Why, to make your fast horses even faster, so mighty Crow warriors can catch the Sioux."

He congratulated himself on that while the medicine man translated in a reedy voice. "The chief says, when you run the match races, are you going to make bets upon the horses?"

217

"Tell him I plan to."

"And what have you to wager with, he asks."

Wiley was getting the drift of this. "Why," he replied easily, "between us we have wealth, gold, that you can trade for repeating rifles and cartridges."

"You will show this to us now."

"Well, I don't happen to have it here. The white woman —"

The chief cut him off with a barked question.

"He asks whether your medicine makes horses go slow or fast. He has decided you will not wager with the Absaroka people. Only run the races. No white man will wager."

Dratted redskins were suspicious, he thought. Not that it made any difference. But let them think it did. He sighed unhappily. "I was counting on a few small sporting wages — just for fun, of course — mere trifles to brighten my day and perhaps reward myself for all this hard training . . . But, of course, if the esteemed chief objects . . ."

It was translated, and there was a long silence.

"No. He who runs the races will not wager. The chief has said it."

"I am gratified by your trust," said Wiley malevolently.

"Now tell us where you are going and when you are going to leave here."

The question caught him unprepared.

"Why . . . back to my road ranch on the Bozeman Road. When Buffalo Tail says it's safe to return."

The Crow frowned and muttered.

218

"We wish to know what you will do there with no more white men passing by."

"Why . . . train horses and wait for better days."

Wiley was annoyed, and felt he was being grilled like some thief instead of an upright entrepreneur. Dratted Indians.

"What horses? Buffalo Tail tells us you have no horses."

"Ah . . . mustangs I shall catch. Wild ones I will capture and train to perfection with my skills."

The lodge grew quiet again. The light through the cowhide was soft. Wiley grew impatient. There were finishing touches to put on those nags, especially the ones he was taking with him.

The chief gestured, and the old translator began. "The chief had a bad-medicine dream last night. The night spirits came to him and showed him the village buffalo runners all running south, led by his own gray racehorse, and growing smaller and smaller in the distance. And when the buffalo runners had disappeared, there was much wailing among the women, for it meant little meat this winter and few hides and poor hunting and great hardship . . .

"And the medicine spirits showed the chief the vision of you on the gray horse, leading the buffalo runners away. The chief came to us, the elders who talk with the spirits, and we listened and knew the vision was true. What have you to say to that?"

Wiley's heart hammered. How could the blasted heathen get wind of such a thing? Had someone talked? Hannah? He laughed easily and drew himself up.

"Bad spirits in the night make jokes," he said. "Your buffalo horses are closely guarded night and day. And I'm here, doing my friends the Crow the favor of making fast horses faster. Won't you enjoy that? Running down the miserable Sioux on their slow ponies?"

There was another long silence while they digested this. Then the other medicine man, younger and potbellied, threw sage on the embers of the fire. It filled the lodge with a sweet scent.

The chief muttered and then turned palms down.

"The chief says his medicine is still bad. From now on Buffalo Tail will watch you, and many others. When the ceremony of adoption of the white boy is done, you will be taken back to your road ranch by many of our warriors . . . There will be no races until after you go. We will run the races ourselves, according to our tradition. The owners of the buffalo runners will run them. Until the adoption you are welcome. After that you must leave our village. The chief has spoken."

The three Crow rose, and Wiley did likewise. He nodded to each and stepped through the door. Cotton-pickin' Crow almost had him. In a whirl he began to revise plans as he stalked back to the meadows. Would they boot him out the morning after the adoption? What time was the adoption? Could he still pull out that night? How many more guards would be keeping an eye on the buffalo runners?

Drat and damn, the hoodoos were defeating him!

220

CHAPTER
NINETEEN

When the sun had reached its zenith on the day of the great ceremony, six village elders, including Two Coups, the medicine men, and Buffalo Tail, began to build a sweat lodge down near the river, not far from Two Coups's lodge.

They hewed supple willow saplings, planted the thick ends in the ground in a circle, and then lashed the tops together to make a global frame. Inside they dug a shallow pit and lined the perimeter with boulders. The women of the village began to heat more boulders in a nearby fire, then hauled buffalo hides down to the sweat lodge for its cover, as well as skins of river water. The medicine men gathered sweetgrass and sage and other herbs, while back in the village, women began to prepare the great feast under the direction of Buffalo Tail's squaw. It was mid-afternoon before the elders came to the lodge of Buffalo Tail to fetch Linc, who had stayed inside, subdued during all of this, some dread mixing with his boyish eagerness to be on with it.

There was nothing for Wiley or Hannah to do but watch. The training had ended the previous day at dusk. Now that there would be no races until the whites had left the village, according to Two Coups's edict, the owners of the buffalo runners had simply claimed their mounts and tied them to their lodges, or nearby, as they always had.

At first Wiley cursed the luck. The carefully collected band of buffalo runners had dissipated, each to its owner. Dratted chief had ruined everything. But then, as Wiley pondered it all, he began to see opportunity. In fact, it delighted him. Instead of having to overcome one or two guards in the meadow that night — the most difficult part of the whole plan — he would simply collect the horses he wanted from the lodges.

It was ideal, except that he could no longer risk taking them all. The more he cut loose in the night, the more he would risk waking up the village, especially if one whinnied. Six would have to do. A spare for each of them, one for Hannah's pack, and one for some vittles and supplies he intended to bring. Drat it, they'd leave behind some fast runners that could be used to catch up with them. If he found time, he'd try to disable them. If not, he'd at least cut them loose and they would probably drift over to the pony herd across the river and be hard to locate in the night.

It took him little time to locate the six fastest horses. He memorized the place of each — the lodges all looked alike in the night, so he took his time about it. And he studied each case to see whether the horse was tethered to a lodge, hobbled, or picketed nearby. He would have to free them all in the black of night and get them haltered or bridled too. Fortunately they all knew him well and would be quiet while he handled them.

222

The Crow ignored him. They were used to the guests in the village now and thought nothing of Wiley's casual peregrinations among the lodges. He caught up with Hannah, who was drifting among the lodges, the same as he was. Pulling her aside, he outlined his plan for the evening: they'd be off before midnight. She would need to have her pack ready for the packhorse, exactly as he had shown her. Unless he could snatch a weapon, they'd have to go unarmed. There was a bow and quiver hanging from a lodge pole in Buffalo Tail's tepee, and they'd take that. Not that he was any good at it, but with any of these buffalo runners, he could close on a running cow or bull and shoot an arrow point-blank.

"But, Wiley," she protested, "you're leaving fast horses behind. Won't they catch us?"

"My dear, trust a professor of the horse. No, they won't catch us. We'll gain ground every day. I'll stake a lifetime of experience with these quadripeds that I have chosen the fastest, strongest, most enduring beasts in the village."

His confidence calmed her. In fact it calmed him as well. It was all worth it. Six good buffalo runners would set him up in business almost as well as nine.

They drifted on over to the sweat lodge now. A small crowd had gathered there. Hides had been thrown over the willow frame, and steam seeped from them. Occasionally a helper-woman would push a hot rock toward the lodge, and there would be a glimpse of the glistening, wet bodies inside as a skin was lifted and the rock prodded toward the pit.

From within came songs, long and plaintive and repetitious, and then quiet, and escaping steam, and the scents of sage and sweetgrass.

Wiley wondered how grown men could endure the steam and immobility so long. He supposed the boy must be half cooked and lobster-red. But periodically the covers were thrown off and the steam escaped, and the cross-legged men within felt the cool sun and fresh air roll over them. Wiley glimpsed Linc sitting between Two Coups and Buffalo Tail, his pale flesh ghostly white and shining next to the glinting umber flesh around him. Well, he thought, the infernal orphan was standing up to it, just like the rest of those barbarians. Probably would end up a heathen like his foster parents. Wiley paused gratefully to think of his own intimate knowledge of the Good Book. Scripture had always helped him in moments of need, especially with a recalcitrant pilgrim.

At long last the soaked hides, black now with water, were stripped away, and the elders and Linc emerged into the long, gold sun, wet and naked. Hannah turned her face every which way and finally ended up watching, as all the other villagers were doing.

Two Coups was making some sort of announcement, giving the new name, Wiley figured. But neither he nor Hannah had any inkling of what it was. Then Linc spotted them.

"New Moon," he shouted. "Yuh got to call me New Moon now." He was excited, and pride shown upon his face.

224

The elders took the boy on down to the river, and they all bathed in its cold current. Then the women threw blankets over them all. The boy had been sweated, purified in body and spirit, made new. The elders had presented him to the earth mother, and sun, and the Great One above, and had named his name. And made him a Crow.

Buffalo Tail herded the boy to the lodge of his wife's sister. Hannah and Wiley followed, along with the villagers. There they dressed the boy in fine new buckskins, a fringed shirt, and fringed leggings of the softest elk skin, and gave him fine new beaded moccasins. Then Buffalo Tail brought the spotted buffalo runner and handed the braided lead rope to Linc. Those who watched exclaimed. They had never seen such a thing! The boy's eyes brimmed. He spotted Hannah and Wiley and tried to smile at them, but he couldn't.

"He gimme the runner, he gimme the runner!" he cried with a delight that was almost anguish.

Wiley was impressed. It was as great a gift as an Indian could give. Dratted horse-thief boy didn't deserve it. All this heathen stuff was getting on Wiley's nerves, and so was this gift giving. No one had ever given him a gift or made some fuss over him in his life.

He nudged Hannah. "Let's go over things. Rehearse this. Infernal redskins have made it tough to get out."

She was reluctant to leave. "It is a very beautiful ceremony in its way," she replied quietly. "I didn't know they had such ceremonies. I didn't know buffalo runners were ever given away. But I guess I didn't know anything about them."

"Come on, confound it. You and I have better things ahead than mooning around a Crow village."

But they lingered on. Linc's new mother, Before-dawn-light, eyed her new son solemnly, and Linc, in turn, seemed to see her for the first time. He peered at his new clothing, the creamy fringed shirt and leggings, admiring them. The leather had been worked endlessly until it was velvety. He caught Buffalo Tail's eye. "Tell her I can't never replace her own son but I'll try, and I got some notion of all she's done for me with these duds," he said.

When Before-dawn-light understood, she smiled faintly, but her eyes were moist. She approached Linc, who still sat on the buffalo runner, and pressed her warm hands over his, and something was sealed between them.

Wiley watched it all, acutely uncomfortable with the softer human feelings, which made him squirmy. The only world he understood was predator and prey. Now, it seemed, the village was absorbed in some ceremony of touching. The whole of Two Coups's people filed past Linc to lay a hand on him, touch him, the contact of his flesh with theirs the seal of brotherhood and acceptance in this band.

Wiley had had enough. He stalked restlessly through the lodges, eyeing the buffalo runners there and wondering what the best way might be to immobilize some of them. There was nothing he could think of short of bodily harm — unless perhaps some locoweed.

But they wouldn't eat it unless they were very hungry. Still . . . that seemed the best possibility. He left the village and wandered down to the riverbank, hunting for the beanlike plant. He was probably too far north; they were more common in the southwest. He circled out toward the dryer sectors, still finding nothing. If he could put some locoweed down those horses, they'd tremble and sweat up and go crazy and be worthless in the chase. He spent a diligent hour hunting, until the dusk was too deep, and then gave up. When he returned to the village, the women were deep in preparations for the dance and feast, and the men had dressed themselves in ceremonial costumes for the dancing, with anklets of jingle-bells, gourd rattles, and hoops adorned with feathers and wrapped in small animal skins.

Wiley watched cheerfully. He and Hannah just might escape while the dancing was at its apex, if the drums and bells and rattles and a hundred chanting voices could obscure their departure. In fact, it might be better during the dances than later, when they were asleep in their lodges and the village was silent.

He found Hannah back at the lodge. "We may go earlier," he said. "They'll build a fire up near Two Coups's lodge and go prancing around it, and the rest will be watching, staring into the fire, and that'd be a better time to vamoose than later."

"I'm not sure I want to go, Wiley."

"Drat it, I'm doing you the favor of your lifetime, and now you don't want it."

She gathered herself and smiled. "That's sweet of you, dear, but I would like to watch them. I like to see Linc happy. I've never seen him happy."

"You're just afraid," he said, taunting her. "All right, I'll go alone. I'll need some vittles. Have you packed any?"

"I don't know what to take," she said, lamenting. "There will be officers at Fort Laramie. I'll need —"

"Leave that infernal stuff behind! You may have to ditch it, anyway."

The woman seemed confused and helpless, and he supposed he might just abandon her. But if he did, he'd have fewer buffalo runners. He couldn't close-herd a bunch of them alone. No . . . she had to come. He wanted six horses.

"If you're going to sit astride, you'd be better off with those split skirts you rigged," he said.

She shook her head, her hand unconsciously patting something heavy within her skirts. He noticed that and decided that she had her gold sewn in there. Well, let her ride with her skirts high, then. He'd enjoy the sight of Hannah Holt's legs.

"Get some vittles," he said. "We'd better have plenty, because we have no weapons. Find some pemmican and jerky. You're a woman; go ask for it."

She stared at him helplessly. "I can't even talk Crow," she protested. Tears slid down her cheeks.

The sight of them astonished Colonel Wiley Smart. The woman was going soft on him, blubbering before his very eyes. He had thought she was tougher than that. Had he misjudged her? Underestimated her will?

228

Angrily he began pawing open the parfleches in the lodge, digging through Buffalo Tail's belongings. It was a grave breach of etiquette, but he didn't care. One contained a boy's things, toys, totems, a small wooden rifle. Another, kitchen things of bone and clay and a few trade items of metal, plus hide-scraping stones that were chipped delicately to the shape of a handgrip. In the next one he found what he wanted: The entire parfleche contained pemmican packed tightly in greasy buffalo gut. He plucked one and sampled it. The pemmican was good, the meat and serviceberries and chokecherries packed in fat and encased like sausages. It was a complete emergency trail food and lasted for months.

"Here. This'll get us clear to Fort Laramie," he said. "We'll pack this on my spare horse and put your duds on one of your spares. You'll be pulling a picket line with two horses, and so will I."

"I can't," she said. "And I don't want to take . . . the wealth of this village. They need those horses to survive, Wiley."

He glared. "Confound it, when have you ever thought about anyone but yourself — especially redskins?"

He had her there. She reddened. And the tears stopped.

"We'll take the six. I can handle mine, and I hope you can handle yours," she snapped. Then she flashed her famous smile at him.

"Now that's more like it."

They packed the pemmican into her canvas poncho, making a long tube with its ends tied. Swiftly now, they carried gear out to the buckboard — the packs, the picket lines, two Indian-made saddles, some hobbles Wiley had scrounged, hackamores, and surcingles.

The feasting had started, and the evening air was heavy with the scent of roasting buffalo hump and spiced vegetables. They walked through the dark and deserted village to the circle of lodges closest to Two Coups's lodge and helped themselves to dripping, juicy hump ribs. It was better than a prime rib roast of cattle, thought Wiley. He devoured vegetable-and-tongue stew, too, spooning it with a bone ladle until he was content.

Hannah had gone to sit beside Linc as she ate, and engaged him in animated conversation that Wiley was not close enough to hear. He didn't want to talk to the dratted boy or listen to his tales. The boy, in his creamy buckskins, seemed preternaturally alive, and his eyes shone.

Wiley feared Hannah might spill their plans to the boy, so he sidled over at last. But she was saying little, mostly listening to Linc's crack-voiced account of the sweat lodge, the old men's prayers, and his naming.

The drums had started then, a steady heartbeat, the hollow, hypnotic rhythm catching the Crow one by one, until their whole attention was absorbed in the dancing. Few of them had eaten; they would dance first.

Chief Two Coups stood near the drummers in his ceremonial dress and bonnet, surveying his village. Wiley watched warily as the warriors spun to the heartbeat, and he suppressed an instinct to vamoose. In

230

another hour the drums would have the village mesmerized. But the clock ticked slowly. He and Hannah exchanged a look. A faint shake of his head told her to wait.

Wiley had expected a bonfire, but the fire that illuminated the crowd was small, and the people were shadowed in darkness and dull orange light that seemed to coruscate upon the lodges. It all looked more sinister and shadowy than it was. Buffalo Tail had joined the dancers, and Before-dawn-light watched quietly beside Linc. One dance ended and merged imperceptibly with another slower one, and finally Wiley judged that the time and mood were right. The world beyond the amber light has ceased to exist for these Crow, dancing through their shadows.

He nodded. Hannah turned to Linc and him. "I'm sleepy, New Moon. From now on I won't call you Linc anymore."

The boy beamed with pleasure.

They slid away into the blue and purple night. The lower end of the village was dark and quiet. The lodges rose like black volcanoes around them. Here and there a horse snorted. It was inky here. Two of the horses Wiley wanted were illuminated by the distant fire; both were buckskins whose movement could be seen in this dark. He cursed his luck and let them go. The others he slipped off their pickets, or unhobbled, one by one, with amazing ease, and soon he had them assembled on the dark side of Buffalo Tail's lodge. They were all used to him and gave him no trouble. He saddled the chief's gray racer, which had been hobbled at the lodge of a relative for the night, and the big chestnut for Hannah. Then he lashed down the two packs and ran long leads to the halters of the packhorse and the spare mounts.

He stared around wildly — his eyes were used to the dark now — and saw nothing. They mounted and were off, the soft clopping of their passage obscured by the distant drums and chanting. He cut west to give the pony herd and its sentries wide berth, and no one halted them.

They pushed through the moonless night, circled the village, and found the Bozeman Road, still without the faintest sign of alarm. Wiley Smart exulted.

Through the rest of that soft, dark night there was no trouble, and when they stopped to rest their horses near dawn, it was at Clark's Fork, and they were well down the Bridger Cutoff and free.

CHAPTER
TWENTY

Five prize buffalo runners and a racehorse! The sheer wealth of it intoxicated Wiley. In any Indian village he could trade just one buffalo runner for thirty or forty good ponies, or scores of dressed robes. He was rich!

At what he judged to be two hours before dawn, he had halted the procession and they had catnapped while the horses grazed and rested. He intended to keep them in prime condition; their lives depended on it. He was troubled momentarily by the realization that he had no firearm. But rabbits had no weapons, either, and like a rabbit, he'd outrun predators. At least, he thought, that's what rabbits usually did, except when coyotes worked in pairs and one drove the rabbit into the jaws of the other.

At dawn they found themselves in dry sagebrush country in the heart of the Pryor Gap. The flat, blue bulk of the Pryor Mountains rose to the east, and to the west, the majestic Absaroka range that flanked the land of the Yellowstone geysers.

There was no sign of pursuit. He broke out pemmican and handed some to Hannah. It had a bitter taste, but it was trail food and wouldn't spoil. She made a face but ate, and then they were off. By the time the sun appeared over the Pryors, a wind had sprung up. It would be a breezy day.

"We did it — we've pulled away, and if the dratted Crow come after us, we'll just outrun them for as long as it takes."

Hannah smiled. There were dark circles under her eyes. She seemed oddly subdued.

"I don't think we have," she said. "You know who'll come after us? Linc. He is so proud to be a Crow, he will lead them. And now we've got hundreds of miles, and Sioux, and . . ." Her voice fell away.

"We'll canter for a while. Get these horses used to running at the end of a line," he said. They did, running a mile before he pulled them down to a brisk walk.

"See that? See how we can make time? Doesn't matter if there's howling redskins behind." He was trying to encourage her. The woman was going mushy on him again.

Near noon he rode to a ridge top near the trail. Nothing. No sign of pursuit. The west wind was fresh and cold, with a promise of fall, but he didn't mind. It blew away the dust of six horses faster than it could form into a telltale cloud.

The day passed uneventfully, and Wiley stopped peering at their backtrail every two minutes and began to relax. They saw no one. The great land of rolling sagebrush hills was empty of human life. He rested and grazed the horses on strong bunchgrass frequently, rotating mounts, so all the animals rested or packed or carried the riders equally. Near twilight they passed the southern flank of the Pryors, and the great Big Horn

234

River basin lay spread out before them, lush with grass. This was the Crow heartland, but shared by the Shoshone as well. The Bridger Road ran along its western edge here but would angle southeast toward the Big Horn River soon.

They camped at a creek where countless other pilgrims had. There was little wood but some bunchgrass on long terraces of white clay. There was debris of the white man here, and three unmarked graves, long humps in the earth. The air was still; the day's wind had died to nothing.

As the amber sun set, Hannah saw something and pointed. Far to the north, a thin column of white smoke rose in a ruler-straight line, tinted red by the plunging sun. A few minutes later they spotted another far to the east, on the flanks of the Big Horn Mountains. And just at twilight, a third, south of them.

"Forgot about their dratted telegraph," he said, an edge to his voice. "I was going to camp for the night, but after it gets good and dark, we'd better put on another ten miles or so. Nothing to worry about. We can outrun them all."

Hannah looked skeptical and frightened.

They rode another three hours and then, weary, dry-camped without a fire. The sleepless night and the pressure were taking their toll now. Before dawn, they were off again. Wiley hadn't slept at all, for fear that his prize horses would be stolen by a lone warrior on the prowl. He wondered now whether he could afford to sleep until Fort Laramie. If he let the horses graze at night, they'd drift out to where they were easy prey. If he tied them close to camp, they couldn't eat much.

It was another breezy day, and that meant there'd be no columns of talking smoke, but neither would his horses leave a telltale cloud of dust. Wiley cursed his weariness. He had intended to dally with Hannah, use his golden powers of manipulation, play on her fears a bit, but she had collapsed instantly in her robe, and he had rigidly kept alert.

The day passed like the previous ones — steady passage through a wide land with ranges of great mountains far to the west and east, and flat, dusty country in between. Nothing. He began to wonder whether the infernal Crow were even going to bother. But something told him they would. The theft of a chief's racehorse and the cream of the village buffalo horses would excite them to utmost effort.

"What will my buffalo runners bring me at Fort Laramie?" Hannah asked that night. They had camped on a murky, alkaline creek in sage-covered hills. The water was barely drinkable.

"Just ordinary horse prices," he said. "I'll take the broncs off your hands for you. What's valuable to the redskins is worthless to white men."

She grinned. "No you won't. I'll find out what they're worth and do my own negotiating, thank you!"

He boiled up, then clamped a lid on the volcano in him. A quarrel, or lack of cooperation now, could be deadly. But one thing he knew: He would take all six nags when they got there. Let her squawk, let her howl.

"You're such a nice man," she added. "I'll trust you to split our wealth equally. Without me you couldn't have brought six, after all."

He stomped away to conceal the wild hatred inflaming him, and felt her saucy eyes on his back. He was tired, sick of her, fighting a deepening dread. When he reached the picketed horses, he examined each minutely, especially their hoofs, and was satisfied. They were a comfort, still prime and ready to race them out of any rising trouble.

When he returned, she was asleep or feigning it. "Miz Holt, my dear Hannah, if you'd like to comfort yourself in the arms of a manly man who watches over you like one of God's guardian angels, why I'm here . . . ready to balm the hardships of the trail . . ."

She was dead to the world. Well, what did it matter? He'd soon be able to buy such delights. He fell asleep that night in spite of his best efforts to guard the horses, and woke with a start in full daylight, panicked by his carelessness. But there was nothing. The six splendid horses were there; some grazing, some standing hipshot in the sun.

There was no breeze this morning, and long reaches of pancake cloud, blue-bottomed, often obscured the sun. The pemmican was disgusting now. They yearned for something else, but that was all there was, and it was keeping them alive and full. He pulled the stolen bow and quiver of arrows from the pack and hoped he might get close enough to some prey to kill it. Not that he had ever used a bow before.

The trail swung south, paralleling the Big Horn River, which was a long strip of green in the distant east. It was a vast, dry country, but the air was transparent, and from any slight rise they could see for a hundred miles. Once they were alarmed by some haze or dust far to the northeast, but there was nothing on the backtrail, and no more smoke signals. The hours in the saddle passed monotonously. They fell into an easy routine, rotating their mounts, grazing them, checking each ridge ahead, walking well to the east of the Bridger Road to leave as few hoofprints as possible along the trail.

That afternoon they splashed across Fifteenmile Creek, which rose in the whitecapped mountains far to the west and wound down to the Big Horn River. They cut a trail leading east, and Wiley supposed it was the one up Ten Sleep Canyon that went clear over the Big Horns. As a road rancher, he had absorbed a lot of trail lore from the passing pilgrims.

By that evening the trail had ducked down into the Big Horn river bottoms, and they rode through emerald grasses and dense copses of river brush, willow, and cottonwood. To either side dry hills blocked the view of the great ranges. The brush provided great cover — they were invisible most of the time even to observers on the hills above the river. But the hills and brush obscured their trail, and Wiley could no longer be sure he wasn't followed. Occasionally he steered them off the road and up a slope to study the land. There was nothing, but some almost invisible dust here and there to the north troubled him.

238

That night he concealed his horses in small meadows surrounded by river brush. If anyone found them, it'd be pure accident. And that night he slept soundly.

The next day they crossed to the east bank of the Big Horn, fording where the bottom was gravelly and water scarcely reached the knees of the horses at the deepest points. Hannah sat inertly, scarcely caring where they were. She had ceased to be watchful. The Crow weren't coming. She felt incredibly grimy and yearned for a bath, even a cold one, but she feared Wiley would spy on her no matter what promises he gave. So she scrubbed herself as best she could whenever there was water and let it go at that.

Late that day the trail left the Big Horn and followed a tributary creek eastward into a white-and-red land of sandstone benches. Wiley paused.

"This is the last of the Big Horn," he said. "But down south a few miles is a giant hot spring with pools perfect for balming body and soul. We could head down there, have some small frolic and medicinal cleansing, and mend bruised flesh in that delicious natural bathhouse. It would be fine sport, after hard days on the trail."

She sighed. Nothing was more tempting now than some hours in a hot bath. She'd feel clean . . . but from the look in Wiley's eye she knew he planned more.

"No . . . let's keep going. The sooner we get to Fort Laramie, the safer we'll be. I'd hate to be attacked in my bath," she added wryly. "But you're a dear man to think of it. Maybe if there's another hot spring ahead we can think about it."

Wiley beamed, and Hannah had a sense of the power of her promises.

They started down the tributary, toward the land of red-and-white rimrock. There were dry purple mountains to the south, and the little creek curved toward them through increasingly rugged country. Eventually they left the creek and started up a long divide over the dry mountains, climbing into a land of purple-and-pink granite and red stone monoliths, all dotted with mountain mahogany and sagebrush and serviceberry.

Two hours later they were afforded a grand view of the backtrail to the north, out across the sun-baked Big Horn Valley. And the sight of it chilled her.

For down there, two miles behind them, was a large party of bronze riders. Too far away for them to discern who they might be but close enough to see there were perhaps fifty on horseback and coming at breakneck speed.

Wiley fairly danced. "Let 'em come!" he said, gloating. "And we'll have us a horse race!" Then he thought better of it. "This pass cuts over to Bridger Creek, and from what I hear, it's a rough, rocky trail, twisting and slow. No place for speedy nags to run. In fact, those mustang ponies'll do better. It's the one spot on the whole dratted Bridger Road where our nags are no help at all. Hannah, my dear, we've got to make time. When we hit the plains down below, near a place they call Lost Cabin, we'll leave them in the dust. But until then . . . it's a horse race."

That chilled her, set her heart to tripping. She thought at once of the little revolver she had lying deep

240

in a special pocket in her petticoat. Four shots — a pathetic weapon against so many. Maybe one for herself. But she was too young to die!

Now they threaded up the divide urgently, past juniper groves and pink granite ledges, pausing now and then to let the laboring horses blow and regretting each moment of delay. The horses turned black at the neck with sweat, and white foam collected around their inner thighs. At the summit they could see nothing — ridges obscured the view of their backtrail. But her every instinct shrieked of danger.

Downslope was slow and jolting. Horses weren't made to be ridden downhill, she thought. At one point she saw their pursuers near the summit and her heart froze. Somehow she and Wiley had lost ground badly. Still, they were over a mile behind.

Hannah and Wiley streaked down the twisting valley that was clotted with sagebrush and red boulders, along a rough, granite path that inhibited running. The buffalo horses were doing fine, but there was no time to rotate mounts and let them rest.

"Fool Crow," Wiley muttered. "They should be grateful for all the favors I did them."

Hannah snorted at that. Wiley's attitudes were unreal. The old mountebank really seemed to believe in his own virtue.

Wiley peered behind him constantly now, and ahead too. Occasionally they caught glimpses of the party behind them. There seemed to be fewer now — about thirty — than what they had supposed.

Wiley drew up.

"We're going to rotate. Be quick about it but not careless. Tighten your cinch. With fresh horses we'll give them the slip when we hit the plains. But first we have to get ourselves out of this creek bed . . . Water them lightly — just a gulp or two."

They reined up. Hannah flew off her saddle, yanked at the latigo, and jerked the wet saddle and soaked blanket off. She piled the blanket and saddle on a big red, but he sensed her impatience and fought the bit as she tried to bridle him. She could hear horses clattering up above.

"Faster, woman," Wiley hissed. "Faster. We're almost in rifle-shot range."

She finally got the red bridled and saddled. And then they were off, with a running start.

The Crow were half a mile behind now and pressing on recklessly. That was only two minutes of hard riding on these twisted, rocky slopes. It didn't seem to matter to them if they ruined horses on the downhill grade, and because of that they had an advantage over Wiley.

Terror gripped her now. She kicked the fresh mount into a jolting downhill lope, and the rested animal responded easily. She drew courage from it. But the other two on her lead line were dragging, slowing them. Wiley's picket-lined horses were dragging him too.

But ahead, only half a mile or so, was the prairie. The land opened wide and leveled into long, clean ridges. They glimpsed it, longed for it, lusted for it. Out there the buffalo runners would burst ahead and run for miles like the breeze. Out there was safety!

A shot racketed behind them, and the noise paralyzed her. Then another pierced the air. She kicked the red horse, yanked savagely on her lead rope. More shots.

"Drat it, run," Wiley yelled. "Kick them."

Another shot, and this time the ominous sound of a ricochet nearby. They were shooting at her!

She made her decision then. She let go of the lead rope, and immediately her big red burst ahead, the spare mounts dragging to a walk behind her.

Wiley saw it. "You damned coward, you've thrown away my fortune," he raged.

Hannah laughed wildly. She leapt far ahead now, racing pell-mell, clinging to the pounding horse as it hit open country and dirt rather than granite underfoot. She kicked it into a flat gallop and howled happily; now she'd make it. Maybe even escape Wiley. She raced easily across the great sagebrush prairie.

And then her heart lurched. Along a low ridge ahead was a line of mounted Indians, sitting on their multicolored ponies and watching the great race. They were armed — rifles and bows and lances and clubs. They were mostly naked, and their faces were daubed with streaks of paint. The one in the center galvanized her. He wore an incredible warbonnet of eagle feathers, with a long tail of feathers drifting to one side. She knew they were Sioux.

There was no place to go. Two hundred yards behind her, Wiley pounded along, still dragging his spare buffalo runners. And behind him and closing were the howling Crow. She didn't recognize any. They were probably from another village. They were shooting at him now, and then she saw him slump and his yellow brocade vest splash red, and then he fell slowly off his saddle and tumbled along the ground as the Crow boiled around him, shooting into Wiley Smart's inert form. Then they snatched his three horses and wheeled back into the Bridger Creek Canyon, fleeing the hundred or so Sioux along the ridge.

"Wiley!" she screamed. "Wiley!"

Hannah sobbed and rode straight toward the one in the warbonnet. She felt the cold, hard weight of the revolver in her petticoat, and it comforted her.

They saw she was a woman and let her come. Her heart thumped so hard, she feared it would burst. Straight for the chief she rode, feeling giddy, seeing life and death, heaven and hell. Then she reined up before him, her auburn hair flying loosely. He was a tall powerful man, superbly muscled, on a great horse. His carbine swung casually toward her until she stared into its dark bore. Other carbines, held by fierce warriors, bored in upon her. She stared into dark, alien eyes and then back to the terrible man who wore the bonnet. His face was expressionless, but his eyes were as flat as death. He looked like Abe Lincoln without the beard.

"Red Cloud," she said, and began to faint.

"*Mahpiua-luta*," he agreed, and let her fall.

She scarcely knew what happened in the following hours. Her mind wasn't in her head. She knew she was alive. She knew Wiley was dead. She knew she was among the Oglala Sioux. She didn't know much more. Her mind mercifully passed in and out of consciousness. She was on a horse. Then off a horse. Someone gave her water. Someone gave her meat, but she couldn't eat. She was not tied, but her arms seemed paralyzed and her legs wouldn't work. They were traveling. She was dead. She was alive. She had to relieve herself and lifted her skirts, not caring.

Then the haze passed, and she lay in a buffalo robe in a lodge. She stared upward — into the observant brown eyes of Red Cloud. There was no one else in the lodge; it was night. He smiled faintly and said something and she didn't understand. He was naked.

She stared and understood. The choice was upon her now. She felt frantically among her skirts until she found the small, cold lump of steel. She could kill him or kill herself. Those were the two options. If she killed him, it would only bring more here and they would kill her. She could submit. She could fight. She could kill.

She dimpled with delight, which bought a moment. Him or her, who would it be? She smiled.

She sat up in the robes and undressed herself. He smiled faintly. She no longer cared what he saw. Under the thick buffalo robe she slid her petticoat off and pulled the little revolver from its pocket. It felt icy in her hand.

She hid it under her. She trembled, and the excitement was not fear but anticipation. She didn't care what she felt.

Then she felt his breath on her cheek, and more, and her hand slid to the small cold gun.

"Damn you, Red Cloud!" she cried, and shot four holes in the lodge cover.

Epilogue

Early in November 1868, Red Cloud and his Oglala rode into Fort Laramie to sign the peace treaty. Hannah was with them, looking gorgeous, saucy, and none the worse for wear in her fine elk-skin dress. Within a few days she completed arrangements to travel east and left many a broken heart behind her at the post. But it was Red Cloud she kissed goodbye.

When Hannah reached Saratoga Springs, she soon became known as something of an eccentric. She bought an estate at the foot of Mount McGregor and called herself Mrs. Red Cloud. In the summer of 1869, she gave birth to a half-breed boy she called Lincoln Red Cloud, much to everyone's amusement. Since she was rich, she didn't care what anyone thought.

She raced a number of fine horses, each with an Indian name. One horse, Sitting Bull, became locally famous. Another, Many-women-laughing, was a disaster, and people cackled at its name. Not that it mattered to her. She began to smoke cigars and take lovers, whom she enjoyed thoroughly and then discarded. She had a great many of them.

The boy, in spite of his mother's eccentricities, grew straight and true, but he could never understand why his mother's face sometimes clouded over when she called him Linc.